BEYOND THE VEIL

VANISHED, BOOK TWO

B. B. GRIFFITH

Griffith Publishing
Denver

Publication Information

Beyond the Veil (Vanished, #2)

Copyright © 2020 by Griffith Publishing LLC

Ebook ISBN: 978-0-9899400-8-5

Print ISBN: 978-0-9899400-9-2

Written by B. B. Griffith

Cover design by Damonza

This is a work of fiction. Names, characters, places, and incidents either are the product of the author's imagination or are used fictitiously and any resemblance to actual persons, living or dead, business establishments, events, or locales is entirely coincidental.

❀ Created with Vellum

To Dad.
For believing in my stories.

Shall any gazer see with mortal eyes,
Or any searcher know by mortal mind;
Veil after veil will lift—but there must be
Veil upon veil behind.

- Edwin Arnold
The Light of Asia

1

GRANT ROMER

My name is Grant Romer, and I'll ride my bike almost anywhere, but I especially like this graveyard. I ain't scared. Pap says I shouldn't play here, even though the whole time I've been biking around and through it, it's been nothing but quiet. Which is for at least a year. Which is a lot for me, since my whole life is only eight years so far.

Pap thinks I'm settin' at Mom and Dad's plot when I come here, but I'm not. Not always. Mostly I just like to ride my bike around and listen to things fly by me, like the trees and the gravestones and the little flags they put in front of the gravestones, because it's pretty quiet here and you can hear the *whoosh* each thing makes when you ride by it fast. Plus it cools me down. In the summer I do lots of things just to stay cool. Pap says there ain't no place on earth hotter in the summer than Midland, Texas. I ain't been nowhere else, but I believe it.

Every time on my ride over I think how Pap says I should stop coming here, and every time I just pass under the Fairview Cemetery arch anyway, and up until now for an entire year of my life it's been nothing but quiet. And this time it's quiet too. But it's different quiet. It's bad quiet.

For starters, there's no mowing sounds, not even coming over the air from a distance where it sounds like not much more than a buzzing bee. And the tons of birds that chirp all day long, they ain't just ain't chirping; they're gone. All I can see is three big crows sitting like drops of mud on the top of the arch as I go under. They watch me ride under them with little ticking movements of their heads, but they don't make a sound neither.

I skid my bike to a stop when I'm a little ways inside. There's nobody here. I mean, there usually ain't a lot of people here to begin with, but there's bound to be *some* people. Not today. I look back at the fat crows, they look at me, then they look down the hill to the center of the grounds where there's a big old house. It's where the graveyard people work. Usually there's a car or two. Now there's nobody. No cars. It's getting on in the afternoon, but it's still a weekday, and during the weekday grownups work even in the summertime, so I know people should be there, but they ain't.

I hear Pap in my head, and he says, "*Son, you stay away from that graveyard. It ain't for the young.*" I think for a second about turning around. But when's the last time you ever had a whole graveyard to yourself? I decide to make my circle. With nobody to see me or get in my way, I get going real fast. The gravestones and the trees don't just flutter in my ears, they start to whine. The air makes tears in my eyes, and they trickle back and behind my head, and I'm smiling, and Pap's voice is gone, and there's nothing in my brain but air that feels double cold 'cause Pap just gave me a buzz cut, and my mind goes blank, and that's why I almost eat it on the rock in the middle of the road.

I swerve at the last second, and my foot slips off the pedal and skids on the ground, and my front tire goes all wobbly, so I jump off the bike onto the grass and roll about a bit until I come to a stop sitting right on my butt. Good thing ain't nobody around to see it. That's not how I ride bikes. I hardly ever fall.

I pick grass from my elbow and walk back to my bike, which looks good enough. I pick it up then look back at the rock. It's glinting in the late sunlight. I set my bike down again and walk over to it and stop. It ain't just any rock. It's a gravestone. Right there in the middle of the road. It reads Andrew Gordon Masterson, and it has the date 1968 on it, which is the born date, but there's no dead date. It has a price tag on it, too. $799. Which is a *lot* of money for a rock. I don't care how glinty it is; that's almost eight hundred dollars. It's chipped on one side pretty bad, and I can see the bit that came off just a little ways away. Like it was dropped there. I wonder if Andrew Gordon Masterson dropped it there, or if somebody tried to steal it, but ain't nobody stupid enough to steal another man's gravestone. Maybe Andrew Gordon Masterson was trying to steal it. Come to think of it, this whole place has that empty, stolen feeling about it, like the grocery store on Wadley Avenue at the end of the week after the roughnecks pick it clean and all that's left is some cans of spinach and pickled things and the ugly fruits and veggies.

I decide to go talk to Mom and Dad about it.

Their place is on top of a low hill overlooking the old house, not far from where I almost bit it on my bike. It's still as hot as it was at noon, but the shadows of the gravestones are getting long now, so I know it must be gettin' on. I decide to sit with my back against Mom's this time. No offense to

Dad or nothin'. I sat under his shadow last time. I like to switch it up.

"What the heck's goin' on here, Mom?" I ask. Don't worry, I know she's not gonna answer. I'm not stupid. I still talk though. Not quite sure why. A big beetle walks slow as an elephant across the top of Mom's rock. I pick it up and set it on the ground. I like beetles, but I can't have them on Mom's rock. It ain't right. I wonder if Pap paid $799 for Mom's and Dad's rocks. They're almost two years old now, and they still look brand new, so I bet they were expensive. No wonder Pap had to go back to work on the rigs.

I can hear when the crows take off from the arch back at the entrance—that's how quiet it is. They come my way, circle over my head up high, and then shoot over to the old house, where they land with the sound of bouncing marbles on the metal gutter at the edge of the roof.

"I think those crows want me to follow 'em," I say. "So that's what I'm gonna do."

I pull myself up using Mom's rock and then slap the top of both of them like I'm giving Mom and Dad high fives. Then I pick up my bike, hop on, and coast my way toward the old house. When I get there I stop hard, and my brakes squeak so loud I think the folks underground might catch a note or two. There's junk all over outside the house. Papers caught in the bushes and receipts smashed into the pebbles that line the walkway, like they were pounded there by boots. A strip of caution tape flutters off one side of the door in what little bit of breeze there is. The front door is closed, but the wood is splintered near the lock. I try it. It opens. I stare inside for a second. The crows nearly set me runnin' when they clack their way toward me on the ledge, walking like stick figures.

"Git outta here," I whisper at them, fluttering my hands,

but it's halfhearted and kinda chickenshit, and I think they know it. Right now I don't mind the company, even if they're birds. One cocks his head at me, but none of them move.

The place has been run through. That much is easy to see, even from the porch. Looks like it was shut down in a hurry, then maybe some kids got a mind to pick it over— maybe somebody like Otis and his crew from up the street from me. They'd do something like that. Or maybe Andrew Gordon Masterson. But Otis and Andrew ain't here now. Nobody's here. This place is hollow. I can feel it.

I reach inside and flick the light switch. Nothing. Which concerns me, seeing as a light's clearly coming from somewhere in there. It's reflecting off the walls leading around the corner to the garden in the middle of the place. It's not a normal light, neither. It's a shimmery, electric blue light, like one of those underwater lights at the swimming pool. It looks like the kind of light that might have run a kid like Otis straight out of this house.

Not me, though. For some reason, some reason that I can't rightly explain, that shimmering blue light tugs at me. It's something I want to see. Pap told me a story once about how sometimes when the weather is just right, lightning doesn't shoot straight up and down. Sometimes it can become a floaty ball. He saw it once, working late on the rig. A floating, crackling ball of lightning creeping around out in the flat desert. He said two men tore off after it in their truck, like moths to a flame, but it popped before they got near it, and it was a good thing, too, 'cause it popped like a grenade going off. Pap said that wasn't even the scary part, though. The scary part was how much he wanted to go after it right along with them. Like he was hypnotized.

That's what I'm feeling right now. I'm one of those

dumbasses in the truck that went after the lightning. I know it, and still I walk inside.

The last sunshine of the day is cutting through the big stained glass window set in the side of the wall to my left, and it colors the floating dust kicked up from all the scattered books and the overturned chairs purple and red and yellow. I walk past a desk to my right that's all pulled apart like whoever worked there lost their keys and freaked out and then just ran.

Ran from whatever's in that courtyard, probably—so I walk toward the courtyard. I'm no wussy. It's been two years since I was really scared, and I said to myself that I'd never be that scared again.

I'm expecting some sort of fresh hell when I turn the corner, but that ain't what I see. It's actually kind of pretty. I walk through the open screen door into the garden, and there it is, floating in the air above the flowers under the sunset sky. It looks like a patch of water in the air. It's shimmering and blue, kind of like a little pond that got lost. I walk slowly around it. It's wide, but it's thinner than paper. If I look at it side-on, it nearly disappears, like the edge of a knife. And that's when I see that something is testing the surface of it. Just little pokes, like a finger trying to push through a balloon.

That stops me cold. Because that ain't right. Nothing about this is exactly *normal*, but the floating pond thing feels like a *right* thing. It's hard to explain how I know this, but I do. It feels like it's got every right to be there, same as the flowers and the bushes. I bet most times it's quiet and flat. But the poking? Nothing about that is right at all.

It's especially not right when I see what I think is the outline of a face pressing through. I can't make out what kind of face because it's still covered, but it's trying to look around, and it's pushing forward here and there like it's testing for a weak spot.

Then it looks at me.

Every hair on my body stands straight up. Even my buzzed hair feels like it stands up a little straighter. But that's not the worst part of it. When I move to the side, it follows me. It sees me. Then it opens its mouth into a silent scream.

What does it sound like? Hell if I know. I'm no wussy, but I told you I ain't stupid, neither—I get the hell out of there. I run as fast as I can. I don't look back. I don't do anything except jump on my bike and pedal and pedal until the wind is ripping at me again and I'm free of that old house. Then I'm under the arch and out of the graveyard. I can hear the crows squawking at me, but they can stuff it. They can keep the graveyard for themselves.

PAP IS WORKING ALL the way over near Lubbock these days so I thought I'd beat him home from the rig, but I lost track of time in the graveyard, and when I get home it's dark and he's reading the *Midland Reporter* on his old chair. The nightly news is on low on the TV in front of him so I know I blew it, missed dinner. News is after dinner for Pap. That's the way it goes.

"Sorry, Pap," I say before he can say anything. He rustles the paper a bit then sets it down on his lap. He doesn't look mad. I've never seen Pap mad. I never want to. I work hard not to. So he's not mad, but he does look tired. And I know it's because of me. But not just for being tardy tonight—for everything. Because Mom and Dad died and I was still around so he had to stop working on his wood things and go back to the rig jobs for money. He's never said this, of course, but I know it. He's pretty old. He should be working on wood things right now, not driving to and from Lubbock and working on rigs.

Pap picks up a small glass of whisky carefully with his four-fingered hand and takes a sip. "Food's in the fridge, son," he says. He calls me *son* even though I'm not his *son* son. He's always called me *son*. He called Dad *son* too, which was sometimes confusing. Back then.

"Yessir," I say, and I trudge to the kitchen to open the fridge. It's fried chicken—my favorite. I'll eat it cold. I don't care. I carry the bucket out to the living room and sit across from Pap on the old bench he made by the window. Our house ain't too big. The living room is kind of the dining room too. And the sitting room. And TV room. I chomp on the chicken while Pap rustles the paper and sips his drink.

"The reason you're coming in so late have anything to do with this?" he asks, tossing a folded section of the paper my way. I catch it with greasy fingers and open it up like a napkin. The front page reads, *Fairview Cemetery Abandoned* and beneath that in smaller letters, *Former customers encouraged to claim their headstones.*

"What's a headstone?" I ask, partly to buy time.

"It's a grave marker," Pap says, looking at me carefully. "The article says ol' Andy Arnaud, who owns Fairview, up and vanished a little over a week ago. Abandoned the whole place. His employees have no idea where he is, but not a one of them'll go back to work. Won't set foot there."

I cough a little as a bit of chicken goes down the wrong pipe.

"Somethin' tells me you are of a different mind," Pap says, which is his grandpa way of saying he knows I was running around the graveyard. I look at the ground. I can hear him sip the last of his drink and wipe the wet ring the glass made from the side table before he gets up.

"Son, I ain't mad about you exploring that place," he says, which gets me to look up again. "I understand the draw. I really do. I just want you to be safe is all. Hear?"

"Yessir."

He rustles my hair and pats my shoulder. The skin of his hand feels rough and strong, and he smells like fresh oil and sawdust. He walks past me and sets his glass in the sink.

"I'm headed to sleep. Don't stay up. Just 'cause it's summer don't mean you can stay up all night."

"Yessir."

He pauses before the door to his room. He glances at me over his shoulder. "You'd tell me if you saw anything there that wasn't supposed to be there, right?"

This catches me so out of the blue it's like I'm hit upside the head for a second. Does he know? If he doesn't, would he think I'm crazy? The last thing Pap needs is a crazy grandson running around sucking up all the money he works hard for. The way he says it makes me think he knows more than he's letting on. But what did I see? I'm not even sure myself. A floating pond? A weird face? You don't just go around saying crap like that. Not in Midland.

"Y-yessir," is all I can stammer out. He nods before going in and closing the door softly behind him.

Pap's got a lot on his plate. Whatever this is, he don't need it too. I make a promise to myself then and there that I won't ever go near that house again.

Out of sight, out of mind.

Right?

2

THE WALKER

It's a strange time to be dead.

Depending on how you look at it, I've been dead either for a year, or for forever and ever, so forth and so on, ad infinitum. The brain tumor got me about a year ago, but what I became has been around since the dawn of time. So you tell me how old I am. You know what? Save it. Let's just go with thirty. A year isn't a long time on the job, so in a sense I'm still a rookie, but even I know something isn't right beyond the veil, in the land of the dead.

I go by a lot of names, Death being the most accurate and the most boring. The Ferryman is another, but I've never been on a boat in my life. I used to get carsick on the rides from Chaco Indian Reservation to Albuquerque General Hospital back when I was getting chemo, so I doubt I'd last long on a boat. Then there's Azrael, if you're into the whole fallen-angel thing, but I'm no angel. Not even a fallen one. There's the Grim Reaper, of course. Pale guy in a cosmic bathrobe who carries around an enormous farming tool. About the only thing similar between me and that guy is that we're both pale, although I didn't used to be. Oh, and we're both barefoot. No robe for me. I was a cop with the Navajo Nation Police Department when I was alive, and I feel most comfortable in uniform, although the one that I wear now is black. No badge. And no gun. I don't carry any weapons, actually. Well, except my fingers. Which I'll get to in a sec.

My bird, Chaco, he calls me Walker. He's been around for a long while and goes by a million names himself, but I call him Chaco because it reminds me of my roots on the rez. He's a bit of a smart-ass, but he generally knows what he's talking about, being as old as time. Since he's the only thing I regularly talk to, I guess I get called Walker a lot. It makes the most sense, too, since my job is to walk the soul map. I find souls ready to go (whether or not they want it is another matter), and I cut the fraying cord of their essence that keeps them tied to the living world. I use my fingers. Pointer and middle. Snip, snip. Go ahead. Try it yourself. Just like that. I tuck the remainder of their soul string back up into the soul map, button up their life story with the stories of everyone else, and then I escort them to the veil.

How do you get this job, you ask?

Well, there's this bell. A special bell. A one-of-a-kind bell that was forged with the essence of the living world and the world of the dead and everything in between. And if I was to ring this bell at the right time, say when my poor brain has decided to crap out on me and I'm seconds from death, well, then I'm spared from death... but I become the Walker. I become Death himself. That's some serious irony, right there.

Don't get me wrong. What I do must be done. But I'm not gonna sit here staring at a soul map full of billions of life forces that I cannot touch until their final moments and then tell you that I don't occasionally get lonely.

One-of-a-kind bell, one-of-a-kind veil, one-of-a-kind job.

The veil is a big, billowing, red curtain that comes in as you're going out. It's freestanding. Like the big puppeteer in the sky plunked down a busker stage right where you kicked the bucket. I can't cross the veil. That's not my territory. I'm the Walker. I inhabit no land—not the land of the living, not the land of the dead, not even the thin place in-between. Only fully severed souls can cross the veil. Most people go willingly enough—some skip, some dance, some sob their way through. Some try to run away. Trust me when I say running never works. The veil follows you, and so do I.

But lately the veil has been... acting strangely. If such a thing can be said of a spooky sheet of fabric. When I started this gig, this was how it went: When someone died I was drawn to their fraying soul string, I cut them free, and in came the veil. The dead went through the veil (or I tossed them through the veil, if they were being dicks about it) and then the veil disappeared. Ta-da! Job well done. On to the next.

But lately things with the veil have changed. I'm losing ground to it. I don't know how else to explain it, but trust me. Like I said, I was Navajo. Still am. Once a Navajo, always a Navajo. I know a thing or two about having my ground taken from me.

Maybe it's best if I just show you what I mean.

I get a tug that takes me to a forest at the base of Mount Fuji in Japan. A place called *Aokigahara*. It's also called the Suicide Forest. The place is known for its silence. The trees here are so dense, they cut all the wind. Your normal forest creatures don't come here. The trees are too thick to run from predators. Chaco told me once that there are certain places that the birds avoid, and at the top of that list is any place without wind. No chattering squirrels, no birds, no wind, dense forest—it all makes for a great place to go hang yourself if you never want to be found.

If you guessed this isn't the first time I've been to the Suicide Forest, you guessed right. About a hundred people kill themselves here every year. Only a fraction are ever found by the living. I find every one. It's what I do.

I step off the soul map and into a bubble of forested silence, like I've dropped down to a garden at the bottom of the sea. The undergrowth is thick. The trees themselves aren't huge, but there are tons of little ones, maybe as thick as my wrist. I reach out and touch one. It bends and snaps back, and it rustles the trees around it, but the sound seems caught up in the canopy, like it was snatched away and stowed in the treetops. I don't immediately see the soul, but I do see a long, satin ribbon stretching out of view.

In the year or so that I've been doing this, I've found suicides come in two camps: those who go through with it wanting to die, and those who go through with it not wanting to die. In the Suicide Forest, if you *kind of* want to die but aren't real sure of it yet, you bring a long ribbon or piece of string along with the rope you're thinking about using on your neck. When you trek off the beaten path, a little ways in you tie the ribbon to a tree, then a little ways later you tie another ribbon, or loop the string around a bush, and so on. There's a ranger here; his name is Honji. It is his sole job to follow these strings when he finds them. Sometimes he finds a troubled case on the other end that he can talk to. Sometimes just a body swinging from the end of a rope. Honji is one of those people who has a deeper sense for the world beyond the veil. A sixth sense, you might say. He is eighty-eight years old. He volunteered for ribbon-duty a lifetime ago, and still does it every day without complaint, and still sheds quiet tears every time he is too late. He is a beautiful soul. In a lot of ways, the color of his soul string reminds me of Caroline's.

This time around, I beat Honji to the punch. I'm drawn by the sound of laughter toward a dense area of brush where I see a fluttering red ribbon. I push through the wall of green, and there I find a young Japanese man at the base of an old oak tree. He's sitting on the ground, hunched like a rag doll in a rumpled suit, and he's laughing so hard that tears roll down his face. He hears me, and his head snaps up. He's smiling. When I come to clip a soul string, I appear differently to each person who sees me. I never know who they are seeing, but this time I must not have looked too out of place, because he still laughs, and it's a relieved laugh.

"After all that," he says, speaking in Japanese. "Everything I did and said, all of the veiled goodbyes and donating everything I own, I jump from the branch and the rope breaks." He wipes tears from his eyes and smiles wider. "And you know what? I'm happy about it! That's all it took! I see now. I see! I can live. I will live!"

He laughs again and leans back on his hands and sighs contentedly, like this was all a big ruse. There's only one problem. I don't get called to big ruses. Something in the quiet way I watch him stills his laughter and drops his smile a notch.

"What is it?" he asks.

I point above his head. There, his body spins slowly from a rope wrapped around the branch he jumped from moments ago. A rope that is very much intact. His tongue bulges out at twice the normal length, red and purple like a cut of pork tenderloin. His neck looks bunched and crumpled on one side. His head rests nearly on his shoulder. He died instantly.

"Oh..." he says, as if he's just scared away a bird he was

watching. He eventually turns back to me, and there's no hint of laughter about him now. "So that would make you..."

"Yep."

This startles him. People are always shocked when I talk to them. It goes back to the movie thing. The ol' point and leer of the man in black. I may point, but I hardly ever leer. Talking to recently dead people is my new equivalent of a Saturday night. I don't waste the chance. It's about all I've got these days.

"But... but... no. How could... how could this happen?" he asks. He's rubbing his face. I think the newly dead still get an echo of the old sensation of touch. He still feels the world around him. But it's not his world anymore.

"Well, jumping from a tree with a rope around your neck might have something to do with it," I say.

"A joke? Really?"

"Sorry." I forget that the freshly dead don't have a real sense of humor. Neither do I, not really, although I'm trying. The Navajo have a... unique sense of humor. When we crack jokes, you can't tell. Maybe it's a joke, maybe it's a grocery list. That's where the humor comes from. If you're laughing right now, there's a good chance you're an Indian.

Anyway, the last thing I want is to become some sort of dour visage of death during the only time I actually get to talk to people, so I'm working on my material with each visit. It's not going so great.

"Look," I say. "What's done is done. Whatever was hurting you back there"—I point up to his swaying body— "that can't get you here anymore. I'm just gonna clip your soul string—it's frayed beyond repair now—and show you through the veil. It'll be all right."

"That thing?" he asks, pointing a shaking finger over my shoulder.

I turn around, and there it is. It startles me, too. "Yeah. That's it."

"Well it doesn't *look* all right," he says, and I can see that he's gone paler still. Paler even than the ankles hanging above his head. And I can see why.

The veil isn't the veil anymore.

It's supposed to be a red curtain. Softly billowing in the breeze, like a rich man's laundry on the line. But this thing is just... wrong. There's a brownish-black color creeping up it now, like the bottom has been sitting in a pool of oil. And it's twitchy, as if a bunch of tiny fists are punching it from behind. This thing looks more like boiling lake water than the veil I've come to know. When did this happen? Come to think of it, the color *had* been changing recently, but I thought maybe it was a trick of the light, or the darkness, or whatever. I go a lot of places at a lot of times. To be honest, after about a month on the job, I kind of tuned the veil out. It's always there eventually. It's the people that I have to be concerned with. The souls I need to cut free.

"Oh shit," I say. Which is exactly the wrong thing to say in front of a skittish soul.

"'Oh shit?' What's 'oh shit?'" he asks, really panicking now. He jumps up into a crouch. He's gone past pale into a shade of milky green, like he's gonna puke. Which would be a first. A dead guy puking. What would even come up?

"It's n-nothing. Listen to me, you have to go beyond the veil. It's what you do. It's gonna get you in the end." But I know my words are falling on deaf ears.

We got a runner.

He springs up and tears off through the trees behind him, leaving his swinging body behind. My old cop instincts kick in, and I take off after him. You'd be surprised how fast a guy can negotiate a thick forest when he's scared to death and he can't quite feel it when he bounces off trees and gets thrashed by branches. Me? I still get winded. I think it's a product of being as close to the living world as I am, even without being a part of it. I get shades of experience and feeling as well. It takes me almost a whole minute of weaving and slipping and shoving through brambles and over a rotten layer cake of dead leaves before I remember, again, that while I might not have him in a footrace, I sure as shit have him beat when it comes to time.

When I want to walk the soul map, I swirl a hole in the living world. It creates a time bubble that I step through, and off I go. If I swirl it just a little bit, it creates the time bubble without the hole. Think of it like a DJ on the turntables, but instead of music, I'm screwing with time. Just call me DJ Time. You'd laugh if I told you how many footraces I had to gut out before I figured out this little trick. So I reach out in front of me and I swirl the space, just like I'm waxing a car. If anyone could see me, I'm sure I'd look like a shitty mime lost in the forest. Everything around me slows, and suddenly the world is my movie on slo-mo, only here I am walking through it all like normal. I'm not gonna lie: this is definitely a perk of the job.

I walk through the slowed world around me, and in about a hundred steps I catch up to the guy. He's turning his head in tiny increments, and I can see that he catches me out of the corner of his eye because his pupils start to pinprick by degrees. To him, I bet I look like I'm moving at hundreds of miles an hour. Like I'm a streak of black light. I stop in front of him, crack my neck, and get a good hold on his arm with one hand. I let out a breath, then I swirl the other way with my free hand.

Time snaps back, and the guy snaps around with it, spinning around my body like a tetherball as I fling him to the ground. I dive on him and pin him. He swings at me, and his fists glance off me. I feel an echo of pressure. Nothing really.

"Hey!" I yell, slapping his face. "Hey! Stop it!" He pushes at my face and muffles my mouth, but I shake him off. "Stop! You're making an ass of yourself, man."

"No!" he yells. "I'm not going in that floating rag! Let me go!"

I fight to pin his arms to his chest like I'm packing him away. "I told you. The veil always wins. Look!"

I point over his head, and he cranes his neck around. There it is. Just like before. Only closer. A lot closer. Closer than it usually is at this point in a chase. I crinkle my nose. It smells now, too. Like dirty, drying mud. I try to keep the disgusted look off my face.

"So you can either run your ass off in the world you left behind until this thing crushes you and keeps crushing you forever, or you can let me cut your string and you go where you're supposed to go."

He stills.

"Will it hurt?" he asks.

"The cut? No. Actually people say it feels like finally popping your ears after a lifetime of being stuffed up."

"No, the veil." I can tell the fight is out of him. I ease up on him, and he sits up, eyes wide with terror. The veil creeps toward him even still.

"I told you, man. I don't know. But it's where you go. End of story."

He drops his hands to the dead leaves on either side of him and lowers his head. "Shit. Just... shit. It wasn't even that bad, you know? What I had here. It just... it wasn't that bad."

Moments like this—when all the shine of sweet release and whatnot is stripped off and these poor souls are faced with their choices and hindsight is crystal clear—they're tough to take. Not much can tug at me anymore, but this does.

"It is what it is." I know it comes out sounding cold, but it's not meant to.

"Easy for you to say. You don't have to go through that thing."

"I know more than you think about the consequences of a single choice," I say, my voice flat.

I think of the bell. I think of Caroline. I think of the last seconds I had with her. The kiss that should have been the first of hundreds, thousands. And I think of my sister Ana, trapped in this job before me. She didn't have a choice. She was only eight years old. She had no idea what the bell meant, what happens when it chimes. How it saves the ringer from death by making him Death itself. "Sometimes one choice can ring out louder than hell," I say. "But it is what it is."

He looks at me as I bring my hand over his head. I make like scissors with my fingers. He nods. I gently grasp his frayed soul string, sick and struggling, like a lightbulb on its last leg. It was strong once and shined like woven silver, but it's done for now. His eyelids flutter in anticipation as I snip it cleanly. Then he actually smiles.

"You're right," he says. "That feels... awesome."

I fold the frayed string up and into the swirled air above him, sewing it into the fabric of the soul map along with all those that came before it. Their experiences form the base of the map. The foundation itself.

"Time to go," I say, and I pull him up. When I turn around again, the veil is three feet from my face. I barely keep myself from screaming in surprise. The guy is tensed under my grip. He's tugging away, and I don't blame him.

I've been wondering what's beyond the veil ever since I got this job, but looking at it right now, I think I can wait a little longer to figure it out. Just when I think the guy is fixing to bolt again, the veil doesn't give him a choice.

It reaches out and eats him. Eats him right out of my hand like a dog would a piece of meat when you aren't watching close enough. One second he's there, the next the veil has swept up and around him, and he's gone in a blink. I pull back my hands like it's electric.

"What has gotten into you?" I ask. I realize I'm talking to a cosmic piece of cloth, but right now it doesn't really feel like a doorway. It feels like an entity. It feels like it's trying to tell me something. The little punches from the other side are intensifying right around where I'm standing. One big one comes out, like a bowling ball thrown against the back of a sheet of canvas, and it's too fast for me to get away from. The veil sweeps out and around me, and I flinch and squint... until it falls back away. It passes through me. I feel nothing. It makes me a little relieved and a little bummed out at the same time.

"You can't touch me," I say, but all the same I back up. It doesn't follow. "I'm the Walker. You have no power over me." I'm feeling cockier now, ten or so steps back. "Nothing has power over me but the bell, you old rag. You got your soul. Now leave."

The veil should leave. There are rules about these things. Guy goes through veil, veil disappears. But the veil isn't leaving. Which is not good, because if this rule is breaking down, other rules are breaking down, and I work in a business where if the rules break down, shit hits the fan. The rules keep things in balance. I don't want to know what happens if the balance between the worlds falls apart. In fact, right now, with the veil staring me down, I'm about the most terrified I've been since I died. Which is saying a lot.

That is, until something pushes from the other side, stretching the veil tight around the five points of what look like five fingertips. It's quick, but it's undeniable. Then they're gone.

Now I'm the most terrified I've ever been.

If you ever visit Chaco Rez, which I wouldn't suggest you ever do without a Navajo guide, you'll see a fair number of Navajo who have just rolled over with what the US government and the Tribal Council give them every month. That's one type of Navajo. But there are others. Some of us, and it's more than you might think, if we're backed into a corner, we can turn the tables by talking. Then there are guys like me, who snap back. The more we're scared, the harder we snap. I think it's part of the reason I was kind of a shitty cop. A good investigator but a shitty cop.

"Listen to me, you piece of toilet paper. You did your part. Now you get the fuck out of here. Take your fingers and shove them up your ass."

The veil billows in waves, almost like it's laughing, or something is laughing behind it. Then it begins to dissipate slowly, blowing away like sand in an invisible wind until I'm alone in the forest. I blow out a big breath.

This has something to do with the bell and the two agents that are on the hunt for it. I just know it. Chaco, my bird, is on the hunt too, and he's a better hunter, what with him being an immortal creature tied to the bell and all, but still, it would make me and all the good people who make up the Circle of the Crow back in the land of the living feel a whole lot better if he just hurried up and found the damn thing already. He says he's close, but the bell doesn't fully present itself until it's found a new Keeper. I told him maybe he should have been a bloodhound or a homing pigeon or something instead of a crow, and he told me that the Walkers never understand. He likes to remind me that, while there have been thousands of me over the years, there has only ever been one of him.

I feel another tug on the soul map. I look around myself at the forest and shake my head in the silence. Duty calls. And this time, if the poor soul doesn't walk freely into that damn veil, I'm tossing them in from a few feet out.

3

CAROLINE ADAMS

I have a hunch that the bell has already passed us by, but I'm still new to this Circle of the Crow thing, so I keep my feelings to myself. Then there's a knocking on the front door of our RV. Owen opens it up, and Big Hill is standing there. I take one look at him and know my hunch is right. It's time to move on.

Big Hill was a swamp bear in another life. If there is such a thing. I'd say swamp alligator, but he's too hairy and fat for an alligator, and he doesn't have near the amount of teeth. He also has quite a soft side. He's squishing up his nose as he says, "I don't feel the bell no more," because it means we have to go, and I think Big Hill has grown attached to us over these past three months. I can't say I'm sad to say goodbye to the outskirts of Shreveport—I was expecting charming and mysterious Louisiana, and this area is more like muddy, backwater, weird Louisiana—but I will miss Big Hill.

Owen looks from him to me then back to him. "What do you mean you don't feel it anymore?"

"I 'spect it was thinking about touchin' down here. But it

ain't thinkin' no such thing no more. It's moved on," Big Hill says in his thick, mumbling, bayou accent, pulling his stained and faded baseball cap off his head and dusting it off with one hand. His chin quivers.

"You mean this thing has a mind of its own?" Owen asks.

"'Course it does. It's the bell. But it ain't here no more, and the Circle, we know the job you've been given, and if it ain't here, you gotta be movin' on." Big Hill clears his throat heavily. It sounds like a downshifting truck.

"Big Hill, are you crying?" I ask, trying to peer up at his wooly face.

"Aw, hell," he says. "I suppose I am. It's just that I like the two o' you." He pulls out a handkerchief the size of a placemat and honks into it.

"We like you too, Big Hill! No tears. You can grab on to your crow totem and walk to us anytime, anyway."

Every member of the Circle has a crow totem. That's the ticket to ride. The crow totems are carved from turquoise and fit nicely in your hand. They depict a crow midflight. They're an extremely old, extremely powerful type of magic... although magic isn't quite the right word for it. More like they're keys that can open up the doors behind our world. If you hold one in your bare hand, against your skin, you can step through the doors for a bit into what we call the thin place. The totem is sort of like a backstage pass to the guts of the living world. The fabric of our world gets very thin, and everything feels much more intense, like you're in the engine room of the world, getting blasted with heat from the furnace. You disappear from the living world as long as you hold on tight to your crow, but it starts to hurt after a while. It's not a natural place for normal, living people to be, but it has its advantages. One step in the thin world is a giant leap in the living world.

Owen calls this type of travel "phasing." Big Hill calls it "blinking."

"Hell, you know it ain't the same as havin' ya here," Big Hill says, folding his kerchief and stuffing it back down the front of his overalls. Owen awkwardly pats at Big Hill's hairy arm. He's trying to be nice and consoling, but he's a doctor. He still doesn't have that one down yet. I'm a nurse. I've got the comfort gene in spades. I step right down to where Big Hill is standing and put my arm around him even though I can't reach much higher than his butt. He hangs his big shaggy head. "Plus," he says, "you'n Owen shouldn't be blinkin' if you don't got cause to. There's strange things in the thin place these days."

"Strange things?" Owen asks, stepping down from the RV to join us. "Like what?"

Big Hill looks at both of us for a moment. I can see he's trying to describe what he means, but he's having some trouble. Instead he says, "I brought you some catfish for the road," and nods over at his rusted-out truck. "Help me load you up."

"Oh... really, Big Hill, you shouldn't have," I say. If I never eat another catfish it'll be too soon. Living at the edge of Big Hill's property, catfish is a once- or twice-a-week thing. Big Hill says he's known all around this area for his catfish. I don't doubt it. If a man his size gives you catfish, you take catfish, even if it tastes like glue.

"No, no," Big Hill says modestly. "Think nothing of it. It's a partin' gift from Big Hill."

We've only met two Circle members so far. I'm told it's because they're very private on the whole. The first we met was Joey Flatwood. Before Ben Dejooli died, Joey was his best friend. Ben's dead but not really *gone* gone—he's the Walker now—so maybe they're still best friends. You never know with Ben. Things with him are... complicated. The first time Joey showed up was on a vintage motorcycle, druggie-thin, wearing a leather jacket that swallowed him up and an Indian hair braid that went down to where his butt would have been if he had enough meat on him to *have* a butt. The first time I saw him, in Ben's hospital room, I wasn't sure whether he was there to rob us or kill us. Turns out he was there to fight for us.

Joey is very, very good at phasing and at using the crow in general. Owen and I are still new at it. When we walk in the thin place, it hurts us. It's a slow, steady pain that increases, like something's scraping at your teeth, until you let go of the crow and blink back. Not Joey. Joey could run across the country in no time flat if he wanted to. Of course, he paid a price for it. He pumped himself full of painkillers in order to stand the pain and get as good at phasing as he is. We've seen him a handful of times since that showdown back in Ben's hospital room, and at first he was completely addicted. I could see it in his smoke. His addiction rolled off his skin in putrid green and weeping yellow. He knew I could see it, too. He knows about my little gift. He just didn't care. He said he had a higher calling and that using the crow to its full potential was more important than his own health.

I told him if he was really devoted to that higher calling, he'd be able to do it without drugs. If you really want to rile up a young Navajo man, all you gotta do is suggest that he's too scared to do something. Works like a charm. I know because I worked with the Navajo for years at the Chaco Health Clinic. Here's another pro tip: this strategy is not limited to young Navajo men.

Recently Joey's been looking a lot better. Stronger. Healthier. His smoke shows up pearl white now when he talks about what the Circle must do, how we are to protect the bell at all costs. *Watch after it, and keep it secret.*

Of course, we need to find the dang thing first.

So, about the colors. If you're the carnival sideshow type, you might call what I have *aura sight*. If you aren't into that mumbo jumbo, you could say I just have a really, really good bead on people. I'm a heck of a nurse. I was back at ABQ Medical and Chaco Health Clinic, and I am now as a travel nurse. Not to toot my own horn, but everywhere I go people want me to stay and work full time. It's not because I have endless patience or because I'm super medically inclined like Owen is; it's because I see what is wrong with people. Literally, I can see it, in colors that come off of them like misty breath on a cold day. It makes for a lot of awkward conversations with Owen when I can see how he's feeling about the road warrior life he took on with me. And how he feels about me in general. Which is, in a word, strongly.

"Here," Big Hill says, shifting a Styrofoam cooler to the edge of the rusted bed of his truck. "Take one end of this and hold tight, hear? This'n is a live one. And a big sucker. You save this'n for a special time with your lady."

Owen blushes wildly, his face turning almost as red as his hair. I can't help but smile. He looks like a deer in headlights, still. As if I didn't know what he was feeling. It was pretty clear that he was falling for me when he asked if he could join me on the hunt for the Keeper. He didn't do it because he loves RVing.

But Owen and I aren't together. Or sleeping together. Or even hooking up. No heavy petting. No light petting. We almost kissed once after I'd had a bit too much of Big Hill's moonshine, which I think is just radiator fluid mixed with grain alcohol. I pulled out of the Kiss That Never Happened. Owen said he understood. He knows how I felt about Ben, which is funny, because *I* don't even know for sure how I felt about Ben. How I feel about him still. All I know is I didn't get enough time with Ben. But Owen understands. He always "understands." He's always willing to "give me as much time as I need." He's always concerned that he doesn't "make it weird." He just wants me to know that he's "here for me." And the bell, of course. But mostly me, I think.

It's not that I don't think he's attractive. He is. He's smart and trim and always well dressed and professional, and when he's in doctor mode he straight-up kicks butt. He's good enough to be a full-blown partner at a top clinic somewhere in the Boston circuit or up in Rochester at the Mayo Clinic, to say nothing of these tiny temp offices we ended up working in Shreveport so that we could keep up pretenses and not completely bleed money. He's the best doctor any of these joints have ever seen. That's his world, and he is the king of it. But outside of his world he's completely lost. His fire puffs away, and he becomes the ultimate nice guy, which isn't all bad, but sometimes it drives me nuts.

The fish bucks in the cooler, and both men pause to steady it. After a moment's stillness, Big Hill nods. They load it into the underbelly of the RV.

"It's packed in ice, but sometimes they still kick. The good ones, anyway. Got a couple more things for your journey," he says, and motions Owen back to the truck bed.

"Where did it go?" Owen asks. "The bell. If it's not here, any idea where it went? Should we just start driving?"

Big Hill walks around to the passenger-side door and opens it with a squeal. I think I can see the rust flake down from the joints. "Follow your crow totem, 'course."

I absently reach for my jeans pocket, where I keep my crow. "I still don't know what these things are, Big Hill. Neither you nor Joey can give me a straight answer."

Big Hill steps back from the back seat, and he holds his hands behind his back as if he's stepped up in front of the class.

"They the stuff o' the vein o' the earth," Big Hill says.

"You keep saying that, but what is the vein of the earth?" Owen asks.

"Ain't seen it m'self. But it's where they came from. Now. Guess what's in my right hand."

Owen sighs. Big Hill is tough to understand when he's talking about swamp fishing, much less opining on the powers that hold the balance between worlds. He takes it for granted that there's a bell out there with the power over death. But Owen is in the business of facts. Diagnosis. Science. That a rock carved into the shape of a crow could defy the laws of physics bothers him a great deal. Not Big Hill. Big Hill wants us to guess what's behind his back.

"More catfish?" I guess, trying to hide a cringe.

"Nah, you got plenty in the icebox. It's a jug of 'shine!" He pulls his right hand in front of him, and in it is a bell jar of grainy moonshine. It looks like pond water distilled through a sock. It gives me a hangover just to see it.

"Guess what's in my left hand," Big Hill says, still grinning. I already know. I can see it coming off of him in waves. He's an open book, Big Hill.

"More moonshine?" I guess.

"How the hell did you know!" he says, laughing loudly. "You're a special one. Both of you are. A jug for each of you. Least I could do for the ones the Walker chose."

I take my moonshine. I can smell it through the glass. Big Hill says the two of us are the only members of the Circle in living memory to have received their crows from the Walker himself. They think this makes us special. I tried to tell him how Ben was just a patient of mine, and of

Owen's. He won't have it. Ben's the Walker. As far as he's concerned, Ben was never anything else. He's right, and he's wrong. Ben is the Walker, but he was much more. To me.

"Now go," Big Hill says. "'Fore I start bawlin' again. Head west. That's as good as I got."

Owen nods. He feels the tug, too, just like I do. The bell is somewhere west. Big Hill hugs us each for a suffocating few seconds, then he practically pushes us up the steps of the RV. "G'on now. Get gone. And remember, don't blink. Hear me? There's things in the thin place. Things watching. Things that shouldn't be there. It's not safe."

Owen settles behind the wheel, wider around than he is. I stand at the top of the stairs.

"Thanks, Big Hill, for everything. Be seeing ya."

Big Hill has his handkerchief out again. He blows loudly into and nods. "I hope so," he says.

4

GRANT ROMER

The city of Midland is different from the outskirts where Pap and I live. The city has a lot going on, what with people walking around in suits and driving all sorts of nice cars and carrying briefcases during the day. I asked Pap one day how many people were in Midland, and he said feels like twice as many after each boom and half as many after each bust, by which he means oil, of course. We're in a boom right now. There are people everywhere.

I feel best in quiet places like the graveyard, but I ain't never going back there, so I gotta find a new place to ride. I suppose I could cruise the neighborhood, but I've done that a million times already and I might run into Otis and his crew, which wouldn't be good since I know they'd rather ride without me on account of they think I'm weird.

I'm not crazy about it, but I got this feeling that I should go toward the city. Sometimes I get these feelings about places, like I forgot something there even if I know I've never been there before. The graveyard gave me that feeling too.

It's why I kept going back again and again. I know I'd have gone ridin' there even if Mom and Dad weren't there.

Pap is working hard on the rig near Lubbock until real late, so I have enough time to wait out the worst of the heat and get started in the late afternoon. Where we live is up north of the city just a bit, and if you look out on it as the sun is setting, Midland stands like a big lightbulb in the center of two patches of dark desert. But if you stare at the dark for a while you'll see it ain't really that dark—it's shot through with tiny dots of light. Those dots are the rigs out in the desert, drilling for oil and gas, day and night. Pap is out there on one right now, and even though I know he's too far away, I like to think I could still maybe see him. Like maybe he's one of the very farthest dots to the north. I wave at him even though I know it's a stupid thing to do.

I can already see the line of trucks off in the distance to my left like one long, glowing caterpillar. They're going to the man camp, which is sort of like a city of oil workers that popped up on the edge of town during the boom 'cause all the people had no place to stay. I don't want to go that way. That's no place for kids. I want to go where the people are walking in their suits and with their briefcases. There's a pretty nice street that runs around the big buildings and has trees and grass in the middle and shops all down both sides. That might be a good place to ride. I cut to my right, down a small, winding road that heads off that way. But I must have gotten my directions wrong because after a couple of minutes the road winds back, and by the time I stop and set down the kickstand, I'm looking toward the man camp again in the distance.

I start off again, but this time I go hard right, down a straight street that I know will take me to the city. Instead I hit construction. A big man smoking a cigarette and holding a stop sign shakes his head at me and points left. I have to pedal up another hill and cross over a park just to get back to where I started. And I'm staring at the man camp again. I hit the brakes and skid as best I can. I check out my skid mark in the streetlights and nod. It's a good one. But that doesn't change the fact that twice I've tried to cut right and twice I got nowhere. The long line of trucks is still there, creeping forward. The lights in the rows of the man camp houses turn on all at once. I spit. Pap would hate me spitting, but I figure it's okay right now 'cause I got a problem: I gotta go left. I gotta follow the trucks. And I gotta ride toward the man camp.

Sometimes things work like that with me, when I get that feeling about a place. Maybe it's true and Otis is right and I am weird, but I ain't supposed to go to the right today. I slide my back tire around until I'm facing the trucks.

Fine. If I'm goin' left, I'm goin' left.

The truck caterpillar came along with the oil boom. It's been there pretty much nonstop for a while now. Pap says the problem is that there's only one main road to the camp and the rigs beyond and it's an old road with two lanes, one going each way. He says it worked just fine for fifty years and even through the first oil boom, thank you very much, but the rigs are bigger now and all smart and whatnot and so they need a lot of trucks. So the rigs changed, but the road didn't. It's still the same ol' two-lane road with stop signs and no stoplights, and now there's a hundred big trucks stopping and going at every stop sign. It backs up for a mile sometimes. Stop and go. Stop and go. I bet it takes a whole day for a truck to get from the back all the way to the man camp.

Better to have a bike at top speed.

I whizz past the trucks in a blur like they are gravestones

back at the cemetery. Some of them honk at me, but I think it's just 'cause they're bored. I'd be bored too, sitting in a truck and not on a bike.

The man camp ain't much to look at. It's mostly a bunch of big sheds spread out in rows, like the kind you keep tools and old cars in. Except these ones hold people, and some of them sell things like food and drinks. I've also seen people selling beer and cigarettes out of them, and one has this man who sits in front of it and brings men inside, and I think there's girls in that one that they pay to kiss. But mostly it's just people living. New people come in when they take jobs on the rigs, and old people leave when their job is up or their rig goes away to find oil somewhere else.

I shouldn't be going near the man camp at all, much less at night, but I can't go against that feeling. Even so, I try to keep to the outskirts where big light stands shine down the dirt roads between the sheds like there's a football game goin' on or something. I wish I could go faster, but there's lots of ruts to deal with from the big haulers and there's people about too. Some of them call after me or whoop. Some of them are falling around like zombies, and I know they're drunk. I have to make a hard right to skirt a big rut, and my bike skids out on tiny rocks. By the time I get hold of it again, I almost run into two men falling into each other, trying to fight. They stumble around and stop cussin' at each other long enough to turn and look at me.

"Hey!" one yells, his eyes puffy and his mouth open. "Git over here, kid!" But I'm already gone. I kick up dirt and rocks behind me and pedal as hard as I can. I hear a whistle by my ear, and a beer bottle explodes on a stack of crates to my right. I pedal harder. I hear a flat-footed thumping behind me, and I know someone is chasing me, probably for my bike, probably 'cause it's a ten-speed. I ain't givin' it up.

I pedal harder than I ever have before, out of the lights, out of the camp, and soon I'm shooting through the tumbleweeds and out on the hard desert floor in the dark, and I'm basically riding blind. My legs won't stop pumping, even though the thumping sound is long gone now and all I can hear is the clicking of my teeth. Without those lights and with no moon to speak of, it's as dark as a basement out here, and I'm praying I don't hit a pothole or a rattler den or fly into a ditch.

By the time I get my legs to stop, I'm way out, like I'm floating in the middle of a lake at night. The camp is behind me, but it looks like a blob of light in the distance. There's a working rig ahead, about the length of my finger. I can see the gas flare like a dancing yellow hat on top of the derrick. There's some clanking, and the revving sound of a big engine floats softly over to me, but other than that, it's quiet. Which is good. Out here, in the dark, what you don't want to hear is rattling. I was snake bit once two years ago, but it wasn't a rattler. Got me right in the crook of my elbow. If it had been a rattler, even a baby rattler, I'd have been dead. Especially a baby rattler. They're the worst 'cause they don't know when to let go.

I shouldn't have started on about snakes because there's a rustling in the bushes that I bet is just a mouse of some sort, but it gets me up on my bike and out like a flash. Before I know it I'm even deeper in the desert and closer to the rig. I feel better closer to the circle of light it's putting out, so I glide my bike as quietly as I can to the edge of the equipment, and in order to calm myself down, I start naming all the things Pap taught me about the rigs.

The first time I saw a drilling rig, I thought it was a giraffe. I don't remember this, 'cause I was just a baby, but I know it's true 'cause that's how Pap taught me about rigs from then on out, as parts of the giraffe. I see the head of the giraffe, the crown block with its little fenced-in fort way up high that I always thought was like the top of a pirate ship. The neck of the giraffe is the derrick, and there's a cord with a hook moving around in there that makes it look like the giraffe is swallowing. The body and back of the giraffe is the platform, where most of the men are now, hooking pipe up to feed the giraffe. Its butt is the engine, which is farting smoke into the air. Below is the blowout preventer, the guts of the giraffe. When I used to cry about Pap leaving to Odessa or Permian or somewhere to run a giraffe for a while, he'd say not to worry, he'd be back because the guts keep him and his crew safe.

I breathe. My heart is back to normal again. The desert behind me is just as big and just as black, but I'm all right with it. The blood stops screaming through my ears. I can actually make out what the roughnecks are saying on the rig. Two men are talking next to the control shack.

"Had to move the whole goddamn pad, is what I'm sayin'," says one. He's in a monkey suit, but he's carrying around a big black notebook, which means he's probably the tool pusher. The crew chief. Like Pap.

"The whole thing?" says the guy he's talking to. He's in a full-blown suit and tie. Not a rig guy. A money guy.

"I been drilling in the Permian for fifty years, Don. Fifty fucking years. And in that time I've moved pads for a lot of reasons, usually because of a geologist or geophysicist or engineer or some other rock licker telling me they think horizontal pay dirt is a hundred feet to the left or right of where we're standing. That's nothing new to me. But that? That shit was too much. We broke five straight bits."

"Jesus," Don says, pulling his hair back with one hand.

"You know how much five drill bits cost? Not to mention

the downtime on a rig in this basin? We had to push our whole schedule back."

"You think I don't know what the cost is?" Don asks. "We're already near a million over AFE because of this little shuffle job you did." He shakes his head. "A quarter section to the left. For a million bucks. This shit better be worth it."

I can tell the tool pusher ain't used to being talked to by a guy in a suit like that. He steps right up into the guy's face. "I'll tell you what you would have got a quarter section back, compadre. You woulda got another five broken bits, at least. I got the drill plan from your engineers. We can hit the zone here. We will hit the zone here."

They keep talking, but I'm not listening anymore. Now I'm looking a quarter section to the right, where the rig broke five bits trying to drill a well. It looks like nothing but a flat spot of black earth under a moonless sky. Like a huge tent was there that just broke camp.

I get that feeling again. Like I lost something there even though it's the first time I've ever set eyes on it.

I leave the rig behind and bike out toward that spot. My bike jumps and bumps over yucca and big clods of dirt. The shocks kick back and forth with a quiet hiss. A quarter section is about forty acres of land, and it's dark as mud by the time I hit the taped-off zone that the rig left behind. The desert is churned up around the old spot and pounded down inside of it. I set my bike down outside of the line and duck under the tape. I don't have a flashlight or a cell phone or anything, so I'm not exactly sure what the heck I think I'm gonna find, but I do have that feeling, and it's telling me to check the place out.

I feel in front of myself with my hands and my feet, like a wall might jump out at me at any time. I trip over a big wheel rut and scramble to standing again. No rattling. That's good. In fact, there's really no sound at all. It's as still as the graveyard was. It feels a lot like the graveyard, too. I look all around me for anything that might look like a blue pool or a creepy hand, but there's nothing. I'm in a pool of black, but it's a quiet pool.

Once I'm where the old rig stood, the footing gets better. The dirt is all hammered down. I can see where the rig was centered. The earth is plated over by a huge manhole. I walk on top of it, and my steps clang out. I jump up and down because at least it's *some* sort of sound.

Then I hear the bird.

I stop jumping like a trampoline's broke under me. The bird's doing nothing but flying, and still it's so loud in the quiet that it sounds like an airplane. It's a darker spot on the black, and I wouldn't be able to track it at all except that I see a streak of red in it that must catch a stray part of rig light that would have died otherwise.

It scares the crap out of me. My feet move so fast I slip on the metal pad cover and scrape up my knee before I can get traction. I pound the dirt back to my bike and slam it upright, but this time I stop before I hit the road.

I've been hitting the road a lot lately when things get scary, which is a chicken thing to do, and I'm tired of it. I told you I'm no wuss. Plus, I don't want to get any deeper into this desert than I already am. It takes all I got to keep my hands on the handlebars and my feet on the ground, but I do it. I scan the flat ground behind the tape until I find it. The bird. It's a crow. And no wonder it sounded so loud coming in—it's the size of a dog. A red stripe starts at its head and runs down its right wing like a racing stripe. The clouds break for a second, and the red glints in the starlight, along with two black eyes. And they're staring right at me.

"What do you want?" I say, and my voice breaks at the end, which is just great.

The crow says nothing, doesn't move a muscle.

"What are you," I say, because I don't need anyone to tell me that this crow is not normal. I can figure that out on my own just fine. For all I know, it might not even be a crow. It might be a monster that just looks like a crow. It stares at me with its beady eyes long enough that I get to thinking about taking up my bike again and leaving this whole mess behind me, but then the crow looks behind its left wing with a slow, steady motion.

"Aw, crap," I say. 'Cause I know what the thing wants. It wants me to go over into that dark where it's pointing. "Seriously?"

The crow looks back at me and nods. I swear to God.

What am I supposed to do when a crow nods at me? I can't *not* at least check it out. Even though where it's pointing is dark as all hell. Darker than it should be. It's dark like a rain cloud dropped right down on the ground. But the crow nodded at me. I'm not gonna bike home and go to bed and wait for Pap to come back and think the entire time about how a bird told me to check something out but I was too chicken to walk through some soupy dark.

"All right then," I say. I set my bike down again. I walk under the tape and over the slammed-down earth and under the tape again across the old pad, going wide around the bird. He watches me, blinks once. I hit the edge of the dark. I puff myself up and walk forward. It's like walking through a mist. I step again and again, hands out, feet out. Then I hear a rattle. I freeze. I step back as slow as molasses. I hear another rattle.

Most rattlers sound like bean shakers. This one doesn't. It sounds more like bird bones banging against a can. I freeze again, but I don't want to, because I know why the bird told me to go here. Why I rode here through the man camp and past the rig. It's because the thing I don't know I forgot is here. Right here. And I know this place isn't what it looks like. It's not just desert. It's where our world flickers in and out. Where things like birds might not be birds. And things like snakes might not be snakes.

There's another break in the coat of clouds, and I see a glint in the desert dirt about ten feet from me. It looks like a piece of tinfoil. I want to step toward it; I feel like I *need* to step toward it. Like every bike ride I've ever had led me to this moment, where I'm just a step away. Two steps at most. I move toward it. There's another rattle, louder this time, and another glint, but this one is like a slick of grease in a parking lot. And it's moving toward me, which I know ain't right. The one good thing about rattlers is that they stay where they're at. Not this one. It's going toward the shiny thing, same as me. I take another step, and it quickly coils up with its head like a floating fist. It looks at me, and its tail rattles hollow, like rocks clacking down a well forever. I don't know why, but I know sure as the night is black that I can't let that snake get to whatever shines in the sand in front of us. I know it the same way that I know I didn't end up here by chance. The same way I know that Pap knows about my feelings. I saw it in his face when he said goodnight after I came back from the graveyard, but I missed my chance to come clean.

I'm not missing this chance.

I dive for the shine. The snake coils back like a spring for a half second then lunges at me. I can see its fangs in the dark. They drip with venom, and I think in that split second how they look like rusty wire. Brown and sick. And they're going to get to me. The rattler shoots forward right at the crook of my elbow as I reach out. I'm not quick enough. Nothing in the desert is quicker than a rattler.

Except the crow.

The snake is inches from the meat of my arm when the crow crushes it from the air. I feel the brush of black wings on my face, then the snake is on the ground, thrashing like an out-of-control garden hose. And it can thrash all it likes, 'cause the crow has it right at the back of its head, and the crow don't look scared. I think it makes a point of looking at me before it snaps its beak shut and clips the snake's head clean off. It even fluffs its own feathers a bit afterward, puffing up and settling down with one claw over the head of the snake. Then it points its arrowhead beak at the glint again.

I dig it up from the desert with my fingers and hold it to the weak light of the stars. It's a silver bell, but it's not. It's the lightest and the heaviest thing I've ever held in my hands.

"What's up?" the crow says. And I almost drop the bell.

His feet are still on the dead snake, but he's looking up at me, expecting an answer.

"You talk?" I ask, then I shake my head. "This is a dream."

Truth be told, I sometimes think I've been dreaming since Mom and Dad died. Like I was in the car with them that night and maybe I'm in a coma. Or dead. It would be easier in a lot of ways. At least I wouldn't worry anymore about Pap. No need to worry if you're just a dream. Somehow the bird seems to know what I'm thinking. And I can feel that the bird gets sad. You ever seen a sad bird? It sort of dips its head.

"This is no dream," the bird says. "And that bell is no ordinary bell."

I look at the silver bell in my hands. As if I needed any proof it ain't a normal bell, it's cold. Nothing normal is cold in Midland in August. I clutch it to my chest. I'm afraid of losing it already.

"My name is Chaco," says the crow. "That bell is yours. It's my job to make sure it stays that way."

5

THE WALKER

We got a Keeper!

Now that the bell has found its partner, I find myself studying the boy. He has in his possession the bell that put me here. If he wanted to, he could off himself and take my job. I know it's unlikely and improbable, but if he wanted to, he could do it. Ring the bell in that space between life and death, and he slips into my role and I fade away across the veil, just like Ana did before me. The thought turns my stomach. It's something I both want and want to run from. Sure, sometimes the job sucks, but other times I feel like I'm a king and the soul map is my domain. A lone king, sure. But a king. Plus, I need to figure out what is happening to the walls between worlds. I can't go fading away just yet.

I trace his soul string, which is sort of the equivalent of rewinding his life. A bit nosy, but who's gonna judge me? I realize I hardly need to worry about the kid taking my job. He has no intention of leaving his world behind and his Pap all alone, even though he thinks, in the shortsighted way that eight-year-olds do, that it might be easier on the man if he wasn't around. He's seen mysteries, too. Places where the world thins. He has a gift for finding them. I suspect it's part of the reason the bell came to him. He has a drive to set things right, even if he can't yet describe precisely why he feels that they're wrong in the first place.

Grant accepts the absurdity of his new job, the realities of the bell and what it means to be the Keeper, in the way only a child can: totally and without reservation. Chaco is amazing with him. For a timeless bird, he's pretty good with kids. I can see why Ana loved him. I felt him calling for me as soon as he felt the bell, and I zipped through the soul map to Midland, Texas, of all places, and watched the finding unfold. If I could have, I'd have ripped that rattlesnake apart myself, but his world is beyond my reach. I was powerless to help. Thankfully, Chaco wasn't.

Afterward, Chaco makes sure Grant gets safely back home. He perches right on the handlebars of his bike, making himself smaller so the kid can see. The whole ride back he talks to him.

"So there's this place you go after you die," Chaco says.

"Of course there is. Mom and Dad are there," Grant says, leaning in close to get a look at Chaco's red stripe. Chaco blinks. That was easy enough.

"And the bell. Let's see. The bell. How to describe the bell? Your bell summons the Walker, who guards the gate between here and there and walks our world keeping things straight."

"Like Death?" Grant asks, stepping off one pedal and coasting back to his driveway. Chaco flutters up and settles on Grant's head. Grant looks up and laughs but doesn't seem to mind.

"Yeah, sort of, but he's not such a bad guy. He's here right now," Chaco says, before *tsking* at himself. Way to go, bird.

Just tell the kid that Death Walking is right next to him, why don'tcha.

"He's here right now? Awesome!"

Chaco looks at me. I shake my head, but I can't help smiling.

"Yeah, he's right there." Chaco points with one wing. "But you can't see him. Only I can see him. He's not always around you, though, okay? And he won't hurt you. He just wanted to see you. Pretty soon he'll get pulled away on work."

"You mean killin' people." Grant stashes his bike behind a bush. He holds the bell tight in one hand, his knuckles white.

"Well, he doesn't kill 'em. He just cleans up their souls after they die. He guards the gate between here and there, and he watches over a map that has everyone's soul written into it."

Grant stares at the empty space I take up. "Makes sense. Somebody's got to, I guess."

I like this kid.

"So... what are you?" Grant asks Chaco.

"A smart-ass," I chime in. Chaco ignores me.

"Well, I go where the bell goes. I'm its buddy. And the bell chose you, so now I'm your buddy too. Like it or not."

There's a little uptick of a smile at the corner of Grant's mouth. I get the feeling he hasn't smiled much recently. I think it's safe to say he probably doesn't have many buddies either.

"You really a bird?" Grant asks.

"Not really. Close enough, though." I guess Chaco doesn't want to get into what it means to be a thin creature just yet. Although I'm pretty sure Grant would get it.

"And you go by Chaco?"

"That's right," Chaco says, fluffing up his feathers a little defensively. I grin. He and I give each other a lot of shit, but I gave him that name, and he likes it. That little flutter says a lot, coming from a thing that has had a million names.

"It's a good name," Grant says.

"So's Grant."

And just like that, Chaco and Grant are buddies.

Grant's soul thread, like every thread caught up in the pull of the bell, is hard to read. Ever changing. Its color morphs from a healthy, shimmering silver to a dusty, faded white and back again. One moment it is as strong as an anchor tie, the next it's frayed and weak. What's for certain is that his life has become a good bit more dangerous than it was when he woke up this morning. And also a hell of a lot more interesting.

I wince a little when I feel that little pricking that tells me it's time to go back to work, and not just because I want to stick around and hang out with Chaco and Grant, even if it's essentially watching them through the window. I wince because it's getting so that every time I hit the scene to clip a soul, it's a dice roll as to whether or not what I see is in my job description. More and more I'm coming up craps. In short, the weird shit is getting weirder.

But work waits for no man. I turn away from our new Keeper, swirl open the soul map, and step through. When I walk the map it's like I'm walking along a massive rope made up of countless smaller strings weaving in and around and through each other. These are the souls of every living person. Think of it like a cross section of a massive fiber-optic cable—millions of points of light that shine and pulse with life, which makes it easy to find the departed soul. It looks like a flickering, broken pixel on a big-screen TV. I zip over to it, stop there, and stand still on the rope.

Something doesn't look right.

Soul strings on their way out look weathered, like creeping vines in winter. This one looks young, but it flickers nonetheless. It's unnatural. It puts me on edge. But it still needs tending to, so I take a deep breath, sweep open the living world, and step off the map and back to earth.

I don't know what I'm expecting. A murder scene, maybe. An atrocity. Or perhaps something just as staggering but on a small scale, like an infant, cold in its crib. What I get is a woman sitting on a park bench on the Strip outside of the Palazzio Casino in Las Vegas, Nevada.

Now, I've paid more than my fair share of visits to Las Vegas. Trust me. This place is like Grand Central Station for me. But this time is different, and I immediately know it's wrong. She's holding a map of the Strip, and she's asking people walking by for directions. People who no longer see her. People who can never answer her. She's older, perhaps sixty, but she looks healthy. In fact, she's wearing beads and a frilly sash and a dress that sparkles, along with running shoes. A yard glass of beer sits next to a cheap, tattered sombrero at her feet. She looks like she's been trying to get the attention of the world she left behind for some time; she's sat down with the effort of it. That's strange in and of itself. I'm usually on the scene moments after death.

"Excuse me?" she says, lifting her arm at a passing couple before letting it flop back to her lap. She looks drunk and in shock. And her soul thread isn't right at all. It's done for, all right, but not like I've ever seen. It looks hacked at, like a broken guitar string.

"Please," she says, holding out her hand again as a young woman clacks by on heels, uncaring, unknowing.

"I'm right here," I say, as if I could do something. As if I could bring her back. I've never said it like that before. I don't know why I say it now. But this woman is in pain she can't understand, and I want to acknowledge that.

"Oh, thank God," she says, and she tries to rise but can't. She looks at her legs like they aren't hers anymore. I hold out my hand for her to stay put, and then I move in and sit beside her. Both of us, on a bench, the Strip seething around us and through us. She looks desperately at me and holds up a phone that is an echo of the one she had in the world she's left, which is another thing that's wrong with this scene. Souls usually stick close to their bodies. There is no body anywhere near us. "I can't get reception," she says. "I've lost my friends. We were just at the tables, and then we went to that bar, and then..." She trails off for a second before starting again. "It's a girls' weekend," she says quietly. "We were supposed to stick together. Why would they leave me? Have you seen them? My name is Karen Mulaney. Have they been asking for me?" She looks up at me for answers, and the terrible sadness in her face fogs my eyes with tears. Not because a poor woman died in Vegas alone. Plenty of people die alone. It's because she shouldn't be dead. And what's left of her soul knows it and is crying out in pain.

I have seen terrible things in my line of work. The most unjust, unfair, unbelievable endings to existence you can imagine. They happen every day. But even those unbearable deaths have a *place*. They have a *place* on the rope I walk, which tells me that they have a purpose, too. They may not know what that purpose was, but it was there nonetheless. I know it because when I cut their souls free, their life story fits back in the map same as every other, and the balance of the map holds.

But this is new. This poor woman, lost and alone in Sin City, shouldn't be dead. I know that as soon as I see her chewed-up soul thread. I also know this: no matter how she got here, it's my job to see her across. I look around for the veil. I can see it down the street, coming my way. It moves like a broom, sweeping over the living with no effect, but the dead have nowhere to run. The veil is entirely black now, which worries me, but not as much as the newfound calm it has. It no longer ripples or bulges or flickers. It's as slack as a curtain in the far corner of an empty house.

"Karen, I'm sure that your friends are looking for you," I say, resting my elbows on my knees. "But they're not gonna find you. You're beyond them now."

"No, I'm not." She shakes her head. "I'm right here. They're close."

So is the veil.

"Karen, can you tell me what happened when you lost them? How you lost them and ended up here?" But Karen has lost interest in me. She's looking at the veil. It has swept its way down the strip and is maybe a hundred feet from us.

"Oh, no," Karen says. She blinks rapidly and scratches at her head then all over her body, like the tweakers we used to deal with back at Chaco. She stretches her neck out like she's wearing a rough wool sweater. Her soul string twitches and frays. I can see that it's causing her pain, not physical pain—she can't feel that anymore—but spiritual pain, which, in a way, is much worse. Her soul is rebelling against being here. It's rebelling against the veil. And with good reason. It's been cheated out of its full lifetime of experiences. Karen's mouth is slack, her eyes wide and rolling. I think about asking her again how she got this way. About who, or what, cut her soul line like this, and how, but I can't bear it any longer.

I place one hand on her shoulder, and with the other, I scissor the soul and set it free. The pop is big this time, like the first crack of a frozen lake in thaw. Karen slumps on the bench, and I hold her upright. I'm surprised to find tears rolling down my face, and I wipe them away quickly.

"It's okay," I say, although I'm not sure if I'm reassuring her or myself. "I had to do it. There's no going back once it's as tattered as that. It was the only way..."

The veil has crept up on us. And before I can finish my blubbering, it sweeps over Karen like limp fingers and pulls her from my hands. It doesn't stick around to gloat this time, either. Once it has her, it pops out of this plane. Then it's just me on the bench, my arm resting on nothing but air.

Now that Karen's gone, my eyes are clear and hard. This is really starting to piss me off. Not just because the veil is sick, or dead, or evil, or whatever the hell it's become, and not just because the things that are supposed to be happening in death aren't happening right anymore. I'm pissed off because I have a job to do here and something out of my power is messing with that. In fact, if I didn't know any better, I'd say some fly-by-night poser trying to play Death did a hack job on poor Karen's soul before it was her time to go.

But that can't be right, because the only one that gets to cut strings around here is me, goddammit. Or so I thought. I mean, the evidence was right there. Her string was mangled. She looked like a shell-shocked soldier wandering around holding a limb she'd just lost. I only wish I could have talked to her longer; maybe we could have retraced her steps...

Or I could just do it myself. I whap my own forehead. Of course. When I get runners, I slow time to catch them. Wax left, that's the slowdown move. I do it now, slowly circle left in the air, and I watch the Strip cut to half-time, then quarter-time, then to a trickle. I pull the Strip to a full stop. Then I keep swiping left.

Karen is back on the bench with me, but she's just an

echo of the past. I roll back some more and watch as she pleads in reverse for attention from a crowd that can't see her. I watch as she stands up and walks backward, retracing her steps. I pause. I want to walk through the end of her life as she did. I grab the frayed end of her soul string with my free hand, then I zip in reverse. Las Vegas becomes a blur of colors and lights streaming over me. When I slow the roll, I'm at the bar next to her, frozen in time. She's drinking in the middle of the crowd of friends that she would later think had forgotten her. I start from there.

I walk beside her as I live her final hours. I watch as they pay and leave and she spills her yard of beer, her sombrero flopping over her face. She and her friends walk to the blackjack table at the Palazzio, and she sets a single chip down. She hits a blackjack right off the bat. She cheers, and the table cheers, and her friends slowly pare off to tables of their own as she keeps playing. She doesn't notice. She splits at the right time, doubles down at the right time. She's an aggressive bettor. They bring her martini after martini. She keeps winning. In one stupid bet she drunkenly splits tens over the protests of the entire table. She puts in everything. She hits twenty-one on both hands. The cheers sound muted on the replay, like the soundtrack to her life is playing underwater.

Karen chips out; she's a thousand up. She tips the dealer a hundred. She gets pats on the back. Her eyes are glossy, and her face is red with the win and the booze. She backs away from the table and looks for her friends, but she can't see them, even though I can. They're at the nearby roulette table and hovering around the craps table. One of them stands almost directly to her right, but she misses her. I want to scream at her and point. *They didn't go anywhere, Karen! They're right here!* But this is a replay. There's nothing I can do but watch as she tries to shake off the booze and walk to the elevators. Either she thinks her friends are in their room or she wants to stash her chips. Either way, she leaves the casino floor alone.

In the elevator, she talks with another couple off to see a show. She weaves in place. The couple gets off on the floor below hers, and she exits alone. The twenty-second floor of the Palazzio Hotel and Casino is completely empty when she walks out. It's a long, straight hallway. The elevator bay is in the dead center. The carpet is dark and patterned. The lights are low. Every twenty feet or so stands an alcove with a vase of flowers or a cheap sculpture. I know on cop instinct that this is where it goes south for Karen, but when I look up and down the hallways, I see nothing. There's an ice machine. That's it. But the dread lingers.

I walk beside Karen as she makes her way down the long hallway. I look behind us. Nothing. She stumbles against the wall, and I almost move to help her before I check myself. I look behind us again. Nothing. She stops in front of her door and opens her purse. She fumbles through it then drops it, and her chips spill out all over the hallway. She laughs and curses. And suddenly there's someone there to help her pick them up.

He's on the scene so quickly it even scares the shit out of me. I jump a foot back. Karen was there alone, and in a blink Karen is with a man. I stop the replay with several quick swipes to the left like a teenaged kid pausing a horror flick to mute the scare. Once the world is frozen again, I take a bunch of deep breaths and get myself together. I'm breathing fine until I see who it is.

It's a man in a boring suit, black or dark blue depending on the light, and a white shirt and black tie. He has light brown hair parted neatly with gel. He looks like the kind of man you acknowledge as doing some sort of important job and then immediately forget when you look away. But if you don't look away—if you get a look at his face— then things change. He's bending down, so Karen hasn't seen it yet, but his eyes are completely black and his skin is as pale as snow.

I know this man. Agent Parsons. I know him because he was the one who came to me at the end of my life, thinking I had the bell. He would have killed me for it, had the cancer not killed me first. I didn't have the bell then, but Caroline did. And he tried to kill her instead. Owen took a bullet for her as she passed the bell to me. I rang it, and here I am today. But that doesn't change the fact that this fucker tried to kill Caroline. I spit at him, but it passes through him. I look down the hall again, and this time I see another figure. I'm not surprised. Agent Douglas always travels with Agent Parsons. The two of them are like dogs that lick each other clean of blood.

I should have known. I press play, my stomach in my throat.

Parsons takes his hand from his jacket pocket where he's been holding something. I know that move. That's a move the Circle uses because they often hold their crow totems in their pockets when they skip through space, but I took the agents' crows. I gave them to Caroline and Owen. And yet here they are appearing out of nowhere again. I rewind it several times. I see the telltale ripple. I can hear the *whoosh, pop*. There's no denying it.

Here's the problem: whatever he has in his pocket, it's no crow totem I've ever seen. I know every crow totem, and every member of the Circle that carries them, from Joey Flatwood all the way across the world and back again to Owen and Caroline. None of the crow totems are unaccounted for. They're using something else.

The Circle has been on the lookout for these two assholes for almost a year, ever since they jumped me at ABQ General while I was on my deathbed. Even though I call them agents, they're not really FBI agents. We figured out that much back at Chaco when the Navajo Police Department ran them down with the FBI but the feds had no record of them. Precisely who they are is still a mystery, even to me.

I've been watching them, too. Their souls are warped and hollow, but they still have them, and if you have a soul, I can find you. I made it a point to check in on them from time to time after I stripped them of their totems, just to make sure they weren't plotting again. They spend a bunch of time in libraries, searching old survey maps and flitting through old microform on creaky machines. They have no social life to speak of. They live in extended-stay hotels wherever they happen to be. They pack a single suitcase each with a second suit identical to the ones they always wear, a pair of spare white dress shirts, and several pairs of black socks and underwear. They meditate at night. At least, that's what it looks like they're doing. They don't drink. They don't chase women. They don't thug around. They're like strange monks. In short, they bored me. And I had a shit-load of work to do and a new lifestyle to get accustomed to, so I admit it: I checked on them less and less.

Then one day they were just gone. Both of them.

I found their soul threads on the map, but when I walked to where they should have been in the living world, they weren't there. I waited. I walked a big perimeter, but I found nothing. I searched as long as I could, until I got another tug to get back to work. Four days later I found them again, and it was like nothing had happened—same routine, same libraries, same old maps of new-world

America and ancient Europe, same hotels. The next day they were gone again. This time for quite a while. But they always came back, until recently, when they disappeared for nearly a month. I knew it was too much to hope that they'd died, because I would know, but that's what it was like. Their souls were clouded and obscured on the map. Barely present at all. It was like they were dead.

But now here they are again, at least in replay. And they are both dramatically changed. I walk around Parsons, bent over and picking up Karen's chips, and I'm shocked at how white he is. His brown hair is turning ashen. His face is as white as milk, and thin, so thin you can see his veins through his skin. And they're black, too. Just like mine. The white skin, the black veins, it's what happens when you spend too much time phasing. I'm this way because it's part of my DNA now. With me, it's the new normal. Parsons looks alien. Like the kind of thing that would walk out of a deep cave. And that's when I figure it out. I can't find them because they're living in the thin world. Joey Flatwood had to medicate himself to near death to take the pain of all the phasing he was doing. These guys have taken it even further. And it's taken its toll on them. They look like mannequins come to life.

I watch as she stumbles and rights herself, still smiling, thanking Parsons for his help and cursing her clumsiness. Until she sees his face. Then she screams. Or tries to. In a blink, Douglas is there, phasing down the hall right up into her face, his dead-white hand jammed over her mouth as he pulls her into him, clipping her struggles. Parsons reaches into her purse and finds the room key she was about to use and opens the door. The two of them walk inside her room. Parsons looks both ways down the hall, and satisfied nobody sees them, he closes the door behind them.

I follow the agents into the room, Douglas with his hand over Karen's face, Parsons calmly walking in after him. Douglas looks like an albino pit bull. His jaw is locked. The veins of his forehead are black as ink, and they bulge from the skin. I have a sick feeling in my stomach as Parsons opens his jacket and reaches into his breast pocket. Douglas lets go of Karen's mouth to reach into his own jacket. Karen pulls in a breath to scream. I don't want to watch whatever is going to happen, but I know I have to. I steel myself and cringe.

Then they all vanish.

I scream in the empty room. I stop the tape, rewind, play again. But it's no use. If they phased, I should still be able to see an echo of them, but they've gone entirely. I swirl open the soul map thinking maybe I can follow a trace of them there, but the soul map is in real time. No rewinding allowed.

They're gone. And they took Karen with them. But I know Karen came back. She had to, to meet me on the bench. So I fast forward. The lights of the Strip blink in triple time outside the big bay window of the hotel room. The world continues to turn. And then Karen snaps back, along with both agents.

Karen falls to the floor. Douglas picks her up and tosses her onto the bed. Both agents step back and watch her, like scientists might a monkey in a cage. Cold, clinical, detached. Karen looks lobotomized. Her eyes are open but unseeing. And that's where she dies. Unmarked and unbloodied but severed at the soul. Parsons looks at Douglas and nods. Douglas smiles. I realize that the two of them haven't spoken a word since they arrived. Somehow it makes what happened here even more unnatural.

Karen's soul leaves her body and wanders through the

hotel room in a lost zigzag. She looks around the room as if she's never seen it before. The agents can't see her, but she can see them. Still, she doesn't recognize the men who killed her. She seems embarrassed and tries to start up halting conversations with them before losing her train of thought. Dazed, she walks through the door and out of the room, on her way to the bench outside where I'll find her. I let her go. It's the agents I'm interested in now. They have something that is allowing them to phase more powerfully than anything I've encountered with the Circle. Worse, they have some sort of weapon. A weapon that strikes at the soul. I get up close to them, trying to find any clue, but whatever it is, it's hidden from me. It's infuriating. I swipe at the imprint of the agents in frustration, but my hands pass right through them.

I let the rest of the encounter play out, fuming at the two men who don't seem like men anymore. They look at each other and seem ready to bounce out, but then they both freeze. Their black eyes darken a shade more, like a dollop of ink has been dropped onto their irises. They are frozen for a moment as if hypnotized, and when they snap out of it they blink rapidly and look to each other.

Parsons speaks his first words of the night, and they chill me to the bone.

"The bell has been found," he says. And he smiles. He's so white it makes his teeth look yellow. Douglas nods. They both reach in their jacket pockets and vanish.

6

OWEN BENNET

Since you're already thinking it, I might as well just say it. I'm kind of pathetic when it comes to women. Or, at least, I'm kind of pathetic when it comes to Caroline, who is the only woman I can remember ever feeling this way about. Like I have this raging, five-alarm fire in my chest. Like my heart has at least second-degree burns, inching every day toward third-degree classification, and perhaps it ought to be admitted to the Burn Intensive Care Unit.

What I can't quite manage to do is fan the fire in her direction, see if maybe she can catch a similar spark.

I apologize for that dose of saccharine. Earlier I said *kind of* pathetic. I think maybe we can throw out the modifier here altogether and just go with *pathetic*. But you probably already figured that out when you realized that I'd been traveling across the country right next to her, side by side, for basically a year, and I still sleep on the modified sofa/table/couch in the main room of the RV. That's a pretty big tip-off that I've crossed from a "romantic candidate" into the friend zone. *Really, really* good friends, to be sure, but you can take your *reallys* and shove them up your ass.

How was that? That was pretty good. That was some genuine anger. I've been trying to back out of the "nice guy" corner that I seem to have painted myself into. I know Caroline doesn't like nice guys. I mean, she likes them, because who doesn't, but she likes them in the way you like your favorite grocery bagger at the supermarket. He's just so nice. What a *pleasant* guy he is. Then you're in the parking lot and you've already forgotten him.

What Caroline *really* likes—I would go so far as to say *loves*—is darker guys, with devil-may-care attitudes, who are willing to risk it all, even to die, to make things right. I know this because that's what Ben Dejooli was. Or is. I don't know for sure where he stands cosmically. Which is another thing. How am I supposed to compete with an ageless demigod who can walk the space between life and death and who singlehandedly has the power to set your soul free? How the hell am I supposed to compete with that? I'm an oncologist. Which I thought was pretty cool until I tried to stack myself up against a demigod. Honestly. Ben and I are basically opposites. We even look opposite. He's this swarthy Navajo badass, and I'm a lanky, freckled redhead.

This is the stuff I think about when Caroline thinks I'm concentrating on the road. We've been cruising west at a consistent seventy miles per hour on I-20 on our way to the Texas border. I like to establish myself in the right-hand lane and really own it. We're following crows, which sounds insane, but if you had the crow totems that we have, you'd know it just feels right to be going this way. Caroline sits in the big captain's seat on the passenger side in her comfy clothes, which she likes to call her "loungeabouts" like the

RV was some east coast estate. I love it. It's things like this that stoke the five-alarm fire.

Her feet are up on the dash, and she's flipping through a magazine we picked up at our last six-hundred-dollar fill-up. She'll read it until she starts to feel carsick then put it in the pile with the rest.

When she jumps a little in her seat and drops the magazine, at first I think it's because she's about to vomit, but then I feel it myself. My pocket is hot. My front pocket. Where I keep my crow totem.

"What the hell?" I slap at my pants like an ember dropped there. I swerve the boat a little bit and get a honk from somewhere to my left before I right us again. The crow is still hot. Not burning, but definitely hot. Caroline has hopped up and is dancing in place. She must really be feeling it. Her loungeabouts are pretty thin, which I also love, but that's beside the point. She starts to reach in her pocket.

"No! Don't touch it! You'll phase right out of the RV! Hold up, I'm pulling over."

I flick on the hazards and shift into a long, slow stop on the shoulder of an exit for a town I've never heard of just east of the Texas border. I'm tapping my leg the whole time. Caroline bunches the cloth of her pants around the crow like she's carrying a hot skillet with nothing but a napkin. I see the outline of the totem. It's pulsing with rich, yellow light.

"What should we do?" she asks. "What does this mean?"

"I don't know," I say, holding my own crow off my leg over my jeans. "Your guess is as good as mine. But *something* just happened."

"I mean, should we phase? What if it's like a page or something?"

"We could try." I'm not crazy about it though. Big Hill's warning to stay clear of the thin world comes back to me. I know Caroline remembers, too, because she's furrowing her brow in that way she does when she's weighing options.

"It's really hot, Owen."

"Well, you could take off your pants," I say before I realize what I'm saying. She cocks an eyebrow at me, but I think there's a hint of a smile there nonetheless.

"It's definitely trying to tell us something," she says.

I see my window. Mr. Nice Guy would most likely advise against phasing. It's the sober, rational thing to do given Big Hill's warning, a man who is infinitely more versed in the crow totem than the two of us are.

But Mr. Nice Guy bags Caroline's groceries.

"On the count of three. Ready?" I say. She looks at me with wide eyes then nods. "One, two... three!"

We both grab our burning crows at once and blink out of the living world and into the thin world. The colors bleed into harsh basics, like an over-touched photograph. The sounds of the world are dulled and distant. Things move at strange speeds. Time seems more arbitrary here, less consistent. I have a theory about time in the thin place. The closer you get to the world of the dead, or wherever departed souls go, the less time matters. There, theoretically, it doesn't matter at all.

The pain is slight, at first. The shock of the color switch and the time dilation is more staggering than the initial pain, but the pain is there. When we get our feet under ourselves, it's more apparent. It's like a slow pinch, but you can't quite source it. That's because it's not on your body. It's deeper, past muscle and bone. I reach out to touch Caroline's shoulder.

"You all right?" I ask. My voice sounds like I'm talking through a tin can phone, but she nods.

"This place sucks," she says, looking around in distaste. "We're not supposed to be here. The living should stay in the land of the living."

My sentiments exactly, but only nice guys call uncle. "The other Circle members use this place as a tool. So should we. We're just not used to it yet, that's all. C'mon, let's walk." I hold out my hand, and she grabs it. Then we take a step. We walk a city block in a blink. We stop again and get our bearings. We've left the RV well behind us. The first time we tried this we ended up hundreds of feet from each other as well and couldn't right the distance in the thin world. We had to phase back and walk it out in real time. Now we hold hands. I don't mind it. I don't think Caroline does either, honestly, if for no other reason than she doesn't want to skip off alone in this place.

The pinch is getting stronger. Was it always like this? I'm no Circle pro or anything, but I've phased a few times. It feels like it's getting worse.

"Does the color here seem off to you?" Caroline asks, echoing my thoughts. "I mean, it's always kind of sepia, but doesn't it seem darker..." And just then a black hand rips through the shimmering wall of the thin world and latches on to her hand, the one that grasps her crow. It grips her so that Caroline can't let go and phase back. For a second she stares at it like you might stare at a bad cut in the seconds before the pain hits, then she starts screaming. She can't scream long, though, because a second hand rips through space and clutches at her neck. She sputters. It all happens in an instant.

I try to pull her my way with the hand that still holds hers, but it's no use. The dark arms jut from thin air, but they're anchored somewhere else, somewhere beyond the thin place, and they won't budge. In fact, they're pulling Caroline backward, and the air is bulging around her, straining with surface tension.

"Let her go!" I scream, but I'm trapped myself. I need a free hand, but I don't dare let go of my crow. I'd phase out, and I could lose her forever.

I swing under the arm that holds her neck and brace it with my shoulder, trying to break the grip. I gasp at the touch of the thing. It sets my heart racing with a rising panic, like it's an amphetamine of some sort. I'm overcome with feelings of disorder and mayhem, but I refuse to let it take her. I strain against the hand, against the panic, and against the boiling of my blood just from being in this godforsaken place. Tears come to my eyes because I know I'm going to lose her. I look over at her, and she's turning blue. She tries to shake her head at me to go.

"I won't leave you!" I scream through gritted teeth, and I feel the walls of the reality of this place start to give.

But then there's a pop, loud and clear, and I know someone is there with the two of us. At first he's a blur—he seems to move as fast in this place as we would phasing through the living world. He coasts on a wave of momentum and slams his fists into the smoky black arm around Caroline's neck. I hear a crack, and the arm caves in. The long, thin fingers fog away, and Caroline jerks her neck forward, sucking in a monster breath.

The third man slides behind Caroline and flips to the other side of the hand that holds her crow. He grabs it as he would the hilt of a sword and wrenches it around and over his head. It disjoints, and he moves to snap it over his knee, but it flits back through the wall and disappears, leaving only a trace of black smoke behind it. Caroline drops to her knees, the crow tumbles from her fist, and she blinks back to the land of the living. I follow her a second later.

Caroline is on her knees on the hot concrete of the shoulder of the highway, and she's vomiting. I drop to my knees myself and suck in gulp after gulp of warm Louisiana air. I reach for Caroline. She's shivering uncontrollably. She leans back and sits on the concrete and reaches back for me. I realize I'm shivering, too. And my hands have that soft-blue coloring that I always associate with cyanosis from hypothermia.

"Told you... that place... sucks," Caroline says, and before she can say another word, there's a *whoosh, pop,* and knowing my luck it's nothing but trouble. All I want to do is lie down on the shoulder of I-20 like a dead armadillo, but I force myself to stand.

I nearly faint with relief when I see Joey Flatwood standing there.

"It doesn't suck," he says, in his quiet Navajo accent where he emphasizes every word carefully. "It's getting taken over."

Flatwood repositions his own crow, which he wears around his neck, to rest over a leather collar piece he's fashioned to keep it from his skin. Then he reaches a hand out to Caroline. She takes it and allows herself to be pulled up. "It's good to walk afterward," he says. "Takes the chill away."

Flatwood looks like he's done a lot more than walk since we last saw him. He's bulked up at the shoulders, and now he fills out his leather jacket. He wears jeans and heavy black boots that buckle at the side. His face filled out, too, but in that angular, Indian way that looks cut from flint. His hair is long but no longer greasy. It's braided with beads and two big black crow feathers that flash in the sun.

He looks like a complete badass, naturally, and while I

could weep with joy from seeing him, I can't help but realize that the Indian version of James Dean kicked the hell out of whatever was holding Caroline hostage in the thin place and saved the day for both of us while I was stuck to her hand like some sort of awful figure skating partner. And he's Ben's best friend, no less.

Flatwood is bleeding at the knuckles, but he ignores it. "I thought Big Hill told you not to walk the thin world. It's not safe. The walls are breaking down." He says this without judgment, only as a statement of fact, in that uniquely Navajo way that reminds me of being back at Chaco. And for a fleeting moment, as the cold still seeps from me, it makes me wish I was still there. In my nine-to-five job. A couple days a week at the Navajo clinic. Living safely behind a curtain of my own.

"The crow totems were burning," I say. "We thought it might be a call of some sort. That's why we phased."

Flatwood turns to me, his eyes alight. "So you felt it too! I swore it was burning, but back in my using days, everything burned. I thought it was ghost pain. I didn't get my hopes up."

Caroline still holds his hand, unsteady. She looks like she's been locked in a walk-in freezer. Her teeth are chattering.

"Hopes up?" I ask. "What's going on?"

"The totem flares when the bell's been found. There's a new Keeper. A young boy. Somewhere in the plains of Texas. I don't know where. Those are the visions the crows have given me." Once he's sure Caroline is steady, he gently withdraws his hand. He looks between the two of us, his brown eyes flashing. "You must go to him. You must protect him. That is your part."

"Us?" Caroline says, wheezy. "Joey, we can't even take

two steps in the thin place without nearly getting killed. You should be the one going."

"She's right," I say, even though it burns me. "I mean, look at us. We're rookies. And... look at you."

But Joey Flatwood shakes his head adamantly. "No. You are the Walker's chosen ones. And I am meant to be elsewhere. I have another calling."

"It can't be more important than protecting the Keeper," Caroline says.

"Everything that is done has one importance," Flatwood says simply. I try not to roll my eyes. "You must go to the Keeper, and I must rally the Circle."

"Why?" I ask.

"Because the time is coming when we must fight to keep this world as it is. To hold the balance," Flatwood says, nodding to himself. He tucks one feather-braided strand of hair behind his ear. "Now go. The crows above will lead you. But beware. The crows above are seen by all. Those that would help the Keeper and those that would hurt him."

He looks at both of us one last time then grasps the lanyard that holds his totem. He flips it so it rests against the bare skin of his chest and phases out of existence. Caroline and I are left alone.

We walk back toward the RV, nearly a half mile behind us, not daring to touch our totems again. We're quiet the whole time, walking side by side, but I sneak glances at Caroline the entire way. She looks forward, her eyes unfocused. I keep expecting to have to catch her, she looks so weak.

Once we strap in the front seats of the RV, she lets out a deep breath. The engine roars to life, and I feel the first real measure of comfort since we phased. I wait for an open lane and gun it, and just like that we're back on the highway. As if in answer, a flock of crows soars above us, flying in our direction hundreds of feet in the air like a black wisp of smoke.

After nearly half an hour on the road, I turn to Caroline. "What is it?" I ask. "What did you see?" Because I know she is attuned in ways others are not. I know she sees things in people, sees what sort of mood they project. I also think she can see what state their soul is in. That is both her blessing and her curse.

"The hands," she says. "They... gave me pictures, in my mind." She turns to me, and her eyes are frightened, her nose runny from the cold she's just been through. "I don't know how to explain them." She looks out the window, gathering her thoughts. "They were pictures of chaos. There was nothing else to them. Just chaos."

7

GRANT ROMER

I like having a crow for a best friend. I know it may seem weird that I could get a best friend so quick, but if you knew Chaco you wouldn't think so. He's an easy bird to like. With the guys up the street like Otis and his crew, you never know if what they are saying is true when they say they are my friends. I asked Otis once, and he sort of nodded and said *yeah* but in the way you say *yeah, why not?* Like he ain't got nothing better to do at the time.

With Chaco it's not like that. Chaco never lies. That was one of the first things he told me. I asked him why, and he said it's 'cause he has no reason to. Lying is a human thing. I believe him because when he says he's my friend, it sounds *heavy*. Like it has the weight of a million years behind it. More than that, even, because Chaco says he came around when the world came around. He wouldn't say to meet up to ride bikes and then ditch me. Things like that don't matter to a super old bird. He's got other things to care about. And the most important one of them is me.

My most important thing is supposed to be the bell. I know the bell is important, but I don't quite know if it's my *most* important thing, because I think my real most important thing is still Pap. I told Chaco this, and Chaco nodded and said he understood but that in time I'd come to see just how much the bell means.

I haven't told Pap about Chaco yet. I haven't told him about the bell, either, which I keep around my neck on a metal chain. At first I was afraid that the chain might break while I'm on my bike or rolling around in my sleep or something and it'd fall off and roll away and I'd never find it again, but Chaco says once the bell is found, it's never lost. It can only be taken or given. That makes me feel a little better and a little worse. I don't want anyone to take the bell from me, and I don't think the bell does either. It sits in this little pit in the middle of my chest that seems meant for it. It hardly moves. It's not hot or cold anymore, and it hardly weighs anything, but I know it's there all the time. It feels *right*, like a brand-new fifty-cent piece or a smooth river stone.

When I get home that night, the night I find the bell, Pap knows something is up. But I just can't lay it all out for him. I don't think I have the words. He asks me point-blank, "You didn't go back to that cemetery, did you, son?"

"No," I say. Which is true. But it's also not true because what happened at the cemetery and what happened when I found the bell are connected. I know it. But I don't know how, so I just sit quietly and stare at the ground. I want to look at Chaco, who is outside in the trees, but I make myself look up at Pap. He looks so tired. His shoulders seem to disappear more and more every day, like he's slumping into himself. He watches me for a second and then nods.

"Pap, are you okay?"

He smiles at me and comes over to me and pats the back

of my head, and I breathe in the scent of wood and oil and hard soap.

"Of course, son," he says. "Just got a long week ahead in Lubbock. That's all. Gotta turn in a bit early. Food is in the ice box."

He pads off to his room and softly closes the door, and I know he's not telling me the truth. He's not lying, exactly, but I know he's not *okay*. I know he misses Mom and Dad, and he misses his shop in the garage and the big pile of raw wood he has in there that's doing nothin' but sitting under a dusty tarp. All these things make him sad.

When I open up the refrigerator, I see a small meal of fried chicken. Not the big bucket, just a few chicken strips, enough for me. Not enough for him. I wonder if he didn't eat dinner so that I could eat dinner, and it makes me want to run into his room and throw the chicken strips at his head and curl up next to him in bed at the same time. He's the one that has a job. He needs the food. And if he works just so I can eat, then there's only one thing I can do: I gotta work so he can eat.

I got a plan.

Back when Mom and Dad were alive and I wanted to buy my bike, I didn't have enough money. I thought Pap might give it to me because he was always giving me a secret five bucks here and there, so I went to him and I showed him the ad in the paper and I asked him for it.

"You know how much this is?" he asked me.

I hadn't looked. I just saw the picture and wanted it so bad that when I ripped it out it tore the price off, so I shook my head. Then he asked how much I had, and I told him almost fifteen dollars. Which was all I had in the world, and I'd saved from Christmas and the last few times he'd handed me a five. Pap said that wasn't enough, which I remember almost had me in tears since I was smaller then and I cried more. But Pap said, "Hold on a minute, now. If you're willing to work for it, I'll make sure you get it." So that's what I did. I set up a stand and sold water and pop from a cooler on Cotton Flat Road, which is a pretty crowded street. That was during May and it was starting to get real hot again, but it was still early enough that people were surprised by the heat and didn't bring water or Cokes along on their errands. I sold a lot of Cokes that day. Made nearly forty bucks. I took it to Pap. He nodded and patted my head with his four fingers, and the next day I had the bike at my house. I'm pretty sure the bike was more than forty bucks, or even fifty bucks, but that was when Mom and Dad were alive and Pap still had some cash, and so I think he spotted me. He ain't never called me on it neither. Now I think it's time I spotted him.

I take my last ten bucks and go down to the gas station and buy two twenty-four packs of different types of Cokes and haul them back in a cooler I strap to the back of my bike. Chaco watches my back the whole way. He seems nervous. He says I shouldn't be out running around because things on his end—the world of talking animals and dead people—are pretty noisy. But I keep thinking of Pap going to bed hungry, and it stings me in the heart. If I sell all the Cokes, I'll make my ten bucks back plus maybe another forty bucks. And it's hot out today. I think I'll sell them all. Especially because I have a great idea, which is to post up near the four-way stop into the man camp and sell to the truck caterpillar. That's a guaranteed crowd.

I dump the two packs of Coke into the roller cooler then take the whole ice tray out of the refrigerator and dump it all over the Coke. I rope the cooler extra tight to the back of my bike seat. I test ride for a few feet. If I go slow, I'll have no problem.

Chaco lands on my handlebars and nearly tips me over as I'm riding.

"What's going on here, my man?" Chaco asks, walking back and forth until he settles right in the middle.

"I can't see when you sit right there," I say. He hops up and onto my shoulder and then my head.

"That's not helping either."

"Remember how I told you to lay low? This isn't laying low." I can see by Chaco's shadow that he's looking everywhere at once.

"Pap didn't eat anything last night. He gets paid at the end of the month. That's two more nights he might not eat, or might have scraps 'cause he feeds me first. Well, I ain't havin' that."

Chaco looks down at me, and I grit my teeth because all of a sudden my throat is clenching up because I'm mad-sad again. "He looks so old and sad, and I don't want him to be that way anymore, but I think it's too late because what's done is done and Mom and Dad ain't coming back, and I'm not old enough to get a real job yet so this is what I got." It sort of pours out of me the way the tears usually do, but because the words came out first the tears stay in and I feel a bit better. Chaco is still looking at me. Then he sort of fluffs himself down on my head.

"Are you hugging me?" I ask, smiling.

"Yeah," Chaco says.

"Bird hugs are funny."

"Just go with it."

"Thanks, Chaco," I say, after a few seconds of riding.

"Well, a man's gotta do what a man's gotta do. Or so I hear. But you promise me a couple of things. First: don't sell to the weird guys. You know 'em. I know 'em. If they look weird or it doesn't feel right, you back away. Second: they put the cash in the can, you toss them the Coke. Cool? You're not getting up near anybody." He leans over and looks down at me with that cocked-head stare that I think means he's being really serious.

"Jeez, Chaco. Nobody's gonna kidnap me in the middle of the day with all those people all around." But actually I'm getting kind of nervous. I was just trying to make some extra cash, but the way Chaco is talking makes me think I'm going into enemy territory or something.

"You haven't seen what I've seen, man," Chaco says. "We got a deal?"

"Deal."

The four-way stop outside is just like I expected. Jammed up and noisy with creeping trucks going back almost as far as I can see. It's hot and humid, and all the heat from the trucks makes it worse, plus the whole place smells like exhaust. Perfect for sellin' Cokes. I chain my bike to a tree nearby and put up my sign, and I'm not set up for five minutes before I get my first beep—a big silver eighteen-wheeler with the round back that looks like a medicine pill and means it's carrying water or oil. I glance at Chaco, who sits in the shade of the tree, high up where he can see everything. He doesn't tell me anything or try to fly out or stop me, so I go up to the passenger door. The driver reaches over to push it open. He's a big fat guy wearing an old T-shirt with the state of Texas on it and some faded words I can't make out. He looks all right.

"You got Diet Coke?" he asks.

"Yessir."

"How much?"

"Dollar for one."

"No shit?" He starts laughing then checks the line through his windshield. He won't be moving far anytime soon.

"Pretty steep, boy. But you got the best of me. Maybe I should go into the roadside pop business. I'll take two."

I toss him the cash can. He seems to know what to do with it, plopping two bucks in. He tosses it back, and I dig around for two Diet Cokes, which I toss up to him. He catches them both then cracks one open. "Cheers," he says. Then he idles on another ten feet, and I go back to my stand.

I try not to grin because I need to look all business, but already that's two bucks I made off of cans that cost me maybe a quarter each. Things are looking good. As soon as I pocket the cash, I get another beep. Then another. I get to each of them in turn. One's a skinny younger guy, and the other is a big army guy, but they both look all right, too. The Army guy gives me two bucks for one Coke and says to keep the change. Then there's a bit of a break, but soon enough another beep. I keep tossing Cokes, and in about an hour I'm over halfway done. I got seven Cokes left and thirty-five bucks in my pocket. That's a lot of fried chicken.

I take a break and pull my stand into the shade under Chaco's tree and lean back against the trunk. I wipe my face with my shirt, and it comes away like a mask of sweat.

"You all right down there?" Chaco asks.

"Yeah," I whisper back. "Almost empty."

"That's pretty good. What say we pack it in?"

I look up and try to find him in the shadows, and when I do, I see he's out as far as he can be while staying in the shade, away from eyes. He's not looking at me. He's watching the skies. I follow his gaze, and I can see why. A whole mess of crows are on the horizon. And more still even farther out, like thin black lines of pencil. They're coming in waves.

"Wow," I say. "What's with all the crows? Is that... are they bad?"

"No," Chaco says. "They just sense a disturbance, that's all. But whatever got them riled up could be bad news. Plus, they're basically pointing a huge finger down at us right now."

Before I can ask more, I hear another beep. I step out from under the tree almost on instinct, looking for the truck it came from. One last sale and then we're off.

"Hey, hombre. How about we let this one be?" Chaco says, his sharp black head flitting from the sky to the row of trucks. I get the beep again, and this time I see where from: a shiny white truck a little larger than an ice cream truck about five spaces back. It looks brand new. I take another step forward, and just then it's like the bell takes a step backward, like it's trying to burrow into me. It doesn't hurt, but it feels heavy, and it makes it hard to walk. I clutch at it, and as I do the truck swims around in my vision. It goes from brand-new to hazy and milky, like an old faded picture of a new truck. I blink, and the picture is gone. But I know something is wrong.

"Yeah, we oughta get outta here," I start to say, but my words are slow. I can't look away as the door rattles open and two men jump out. They wear black suits and black sunglasses, but their skin is whiter than the truck. One stands tall, and the other is sort of hunched over with his hands out. Even their brown hair is faded, like their heads were dusted in powder.

They both take off their sunglasses, and their eyes are like black marbles. I know because they're looking right at me. When they see me, the eyes widen, but they're still black all through. I try to run, but my feet don't seem to be working like they should. Everything feels muddled. I look up for Chaco, but I don't see him. That's when I really get scared.

The two men look at each other, and the tall one nods at the thicker one, who pops his neck back and forth and disappears. There's a *whoosh, pop*, and then he's inches from me, his hand out like a claw going for my neck. This close, I notice his skin has black veins and that a turquoise glow comes from underneath his jacket, but all I can really see are his eyes. They say one thing: *I am going to kill you.*

His long fingernails brush my throat, but that's as far as they get. A river of black pours out of the sky, and wings rush all around me. All I hear is the sound of a million feathers along with a fast clapping sound as the birds slam into the man. He staggers back, punching at them with his fists, but it's no use. For every one he hits, ten more are behind. The man roars like a bear, raging forward, and he almost gets to me until one crow, my crow, the biggest crow of all, passes right over my head and rakes him with talons as big as your finger. The man's head snaps back, and Chaco takes a strip of his face with him as he circles up and around for another go, but the man has already disappeared. In a blink he's back with the other guy by the truck, one arm over his eyes.

"Let's go!" Chaco says to me, flapping in front of my face, and it's like the birds are part of him. They flow through and around him like water, like they're his wings. "They will buy us time!"

I flick off the cooler hitch, hop on my bike, and tear away, not even looking behind me, not even caring about the seven Cokes. Chaco is above, just in my sight. More and more birds are whipping by us, all going back at the two men. I try not to think how each beak is as sharp as a razor and missing my face by inches, but none of the crows touch me. Not even a feather. I only feel the wind from their passing, and I try to focus on following Chaco. He's like a living GPS, ticking right and left just before I get to turns so I know where to go. I pump the brakes to skid into turns. I pedal so hard I kick up gravel behind me. The wind brings tears to my eyes, and I remember how it did the same thing back at the graveyard when I listened to the rows of gravestones fly by. That seems like a lifetime ago now.

It took me almost thirty minutes to get down to the four-way stop sign, but it feels like I get back home in about a minute. I stash my bike in the bushes where nobody will see it and open up the front door and turn around and actually lock it, which I almost never do, and then I run into my room and squeeze in the small space between my bed and the dresser. I haven't squeezed in between there since the days and weeks just after Mom and Dad died. It's a lot tighter than it was then, but I still fit. A few seconds later there's a light tapping on the window above my head. I look up and see Chaco there, taking up most of the window.

"You all right in there?" he asks.

I shake my head.

"You hurt?"

I shake my head again.

"You scared?" he asks after a minute.

I nod.

"You wanna talk about it?"

I shake my head. I just want to sit here for a second and hug my knees.

"D'you, uh... You want me to leave you alone?"

I tilt my head up to look at him, and I see him looking down at me. His eyes are sad. I didn't think it was possible for bird eyes to be sad, but his are. I shake my head again, hard this time. He sort of fluffs up, and when he settles again his eyes are less sad.

"All right then. I'll just stay right here, okay? Sometimes you need to sit and chill in the corner for a bit. I get that."

And that's where Pap finds me when he comes home that night. Still sitting in the corner, my knees to my chest. He calls my name a few times, and I call back but it sounds weak and like a baby, so Pap opens my door really slow.

"Grant?" he asks, switching on the light. He looks around until he finds me, then he's quiet for a second, hard hat in hand. "Are you all right, son?"

Everything wells up inside me then, and it's like my head is a full bucket of water that tips over, and for some reason all I can think to say is, "I left the cooler and my Cokes," and then I start crying. I cry so hard it's completely silent. Pap gets down on one knee, then both knees, and then he sits down, and then he takes one of my hands from where it clutches my legs and he presses it between both of his hands, and they're cool and rough and clean. After a minute, it calms me down enough that I can talk again.

"I have a friend who's a bird," I say. I don't know why I say it. I'm tired of holding things from Pap. I never want to hold anything from him again.

"I had a lot of friends like that too when I was your age," Pap says. "I wish some of them had stuck around, sometimes. They were so... I dunno. It's like they were real."

"He's still here," I say.

"Yeah?" Pap says, his voice gentle. "Where?"

"He's right out of the window."

Pap looks up. "Holy Jesus!" he says, and his hand shoots to his mouth because he never says that. I know I should be shocked, but it's so out of place and the look on his face is so open mouthed and wide eyed that I start to laugh.

"His name is Chaco. He can talk, but only to me I think." I watch Pap watch Chaco, and I smile more as Chaco does this funny little bow thing that smashes his head against the glass. "You think I'm crazy, don't you? And a liar," I say, looking down again. "Maybe I am. Maybe this is a big dream, and I was in that car too. I think that sometimes."

"No," Pap says quickly. "No. Never. You're not crazy, and you weren't in that car, thank God Almighty. And you sure as hell ain't a liar. Pardon my mouth tonight." His eyes are still on Chaco. "That is one big bird, son."

"He's probably my best friend. I met him when I found this bell." I take the bell out from under my shirt and hold it out to him. There's no ringer, which is good. It has a heavy shine to it. Not bright or polished. Heavy. I know Pap knows it ain't normal. He doesn't try to touch it or hold it, which I like. After a second, I tuck it back away. "But you can't tell no one about the bell, Pap."

Pap looks me square in the face for a second, and I can tell he's thinking hard, digging deep in his brain. He looks up at Chaco, who watches both of us with a flat gaze.

"Where'd you find the bell?" he asks me.

"In the desert past the man camp. Maybe a half mile in."

"There's the Wilmington rig out near there," Pap says, thinking. "They just moved the pad."

"Yeah, that's the one. Near there. How did you know?"

"Because that's a thin place," Pap says. "A place where things are different."

Above me, Chaco nods. "I knew it!" Chaco says. "I knew it! He's like you, my man!"

I look at Pap cockeyed for a second. "The graveyard is the same way."

"I guessed as much. That's why I told you to keep out. Those types of places, they ain't bad, exactly, but they ain't good either. They're just..."

"Thin," I say.

Pap nods.

"And sometimes thin places don't sit right with people who don't know about them. Now, I don't know nothin' 'bout no bell, but I do know this. You are a special boy. I think your father had some of it too, rest his soul. He didn't get the time to use it. But you're special too. You're like me. You can see the thin places. You feel them."

"They give me this feeling like I lost something there even though I've never been there," I say, and all of a sudden I feel this warm sense of relief. If you ever thought you were going crazy and then found out you weren't, you'd know what I feel like. If not, I just can't explain it to you. It's like something big breaks inside you for the better.

"But you saw something there today," Pap says, his face darkening. "Something scary."

I shake my head. "Not there. No. I saw it near the four-way stop on the road that leads to the camp. In the middle of the truck caterpillar. Two guys. But they weren't guys. They weren't even people like I've ever seen." I look up at Chaco, who is watching me carefully. "And I think they knew. I think they knew about the bell. And they wanted it *so bad*."

Chaco nods. "They did. I'm not gonna sugarcoat this because that's not what I do, so here's the truth. They've wanted that bell for a long time, and they're about the worst kind of thing you can imagine. Now that they know you've got it, they're looking for you."

"What do we do?" I ask, and my voice is quiet and mousey, and I think how strange it must be for Pap to hear a one-sided conversation like this. "If a million birds can't stop 'em, what can the three of us do?"

Chaco spreads his wings, and they shoot out past the edges of the window. "You're never as alone as you think, hombre. Remember how I told you that everyone could see all those crows in the sky? Well, there are people that are as good as those two are bad, and they saw the crows too. They're coming our way. We just gotta make sure it's them that find us first."

8

THE WALKER

All I want to do is go after the agents. I know they're headed for Grant and Chaco. Two pictures float in my mind. The first is Grant, still just a kid, clutching the bell like he just snatched a hundred bucks off the sidewalk, trying to figure out what it all means and what his part in it is. The other is Karen. Her soul butchered—hanging by a thread before its time. Grant could end up like that. And that doesn't sit well with me. The lifespan of a soul is written well before its thread is first spun. From day one, I took comfort in knowing that no matter what kind of fresh hell the agents want to rain down on the world of the living, no matter how thin the walls between the worlds have become, all of it was already written into the souls that play a part. It has been since they were created.

What happened to Karen is shaking that faith. It sure as hell looked to me like what happened to her wasn't part of any plan.

I step out of Vegas and into the soul map and start sifting through strands, looking for Parsons and Douglas again. Even if they were in the thin world and hidden from me, their last steps in the living world would at least give me a clue as to where they were. But when I walk the map in their footsteps, it's like a huge game of Twister. One foot in Vegas, the next in California, then to Arizona, then New Mexico, and on and on. These guys are phasing on a level I didn't think possible, striding across entire states at a time. But this time I'm not going to lose them. I'm tracking them step-by-step when I get called away again. That's me, always on the clock.

I walk the map until I find the flickering soul, and again I stop. This one is all sorts of weird. If a soul is like a shining lightbulb, and a soul on its way out is a dim, flickering light-bulb, then this thing, if it can be called a soul, is a lightbulb that rattles hollow with a blown filament, just a shell now.

At times like this, where I get one weird call after the next, I really wish Chaco was around. But he has a new job now. And it's time I did mine. I swirl open the map and step into the living world.

I land outside of the Albuquerque foothills. Not all that far from Chaco Reservation, as the crow flies. I recognize Palomas Peak to the south and what looks to be a single bright streetlight illuminating I-85 to the distant west.

I'm looking at a man named Stanley Vickers. He's a sixty-seven-year-old accountant who lives and works in Plymouth, Virginia. He has two kids in their late thirties and is divorced going on ten years now. He died of a heart attack while sitting behind his desk.

I know all of this because I walked Stanley through the veil a week ago, back in Plymouth. And yet here Stanley is again, wandering around in the middle of nowhere, New Mexico.

"Stanley? What the hell are you doing here?"

Stanley seems to register my voice, but when he turns

around and looks at me, his face has this slack blankness to it that reminds me of the paint huffers back on the rez. He weaves in place. His eyes slowly close then slowly open again. He doesn't answer me. I walk up to him. He doesn't move. I wave my hand in front of his face and snap my fingers a few times. His skin seems to mist away a little bit, as if he's not quite whole.

"Stanley. Hello? You in there, Stan?" I wave my hand above his head. No soul string there. I shouldn't be surprised since I snipped it myself barely a blink ago, but I snip all around him anyway just in case. His hair and skin swirl around as if they're losing consistency, but nothing else happens. No pop, no release. Whatever this thing is, it's not Stanley. I put my hands on my hips and look around the desert in the failing light.

"Where is that damn veil," I mutter, and sure enough, there it is, gliding toward us across the darkening plains in complete silence. It doesn't catch the light so much as poke a hole through what remains. It is entirely black, and it's as flat and dead as a lake surface. To be honest, it's scary as hell, so I do what I do to all things that I'm confronted with that scare me. I start cussing at it.

"Why don't you do your fucking job, huh? I cut the strings, you take the souls. Where is the major breakdown here..." But as it approaches, I trail off. This thing is nonresponsive. It's as much of the veil I once knew as this shell wandering the desert is Stanley Vickers.

"Are you gonna take him?" I ask, stammering a little. "Look at him. He's just standing there."

The veil doesn't move. I feel like I'm talking to a corpse. But of course it wouldn't recognize him. It already took him once. As far as the veil knows, Stanley is on the other side. It must have sensed the disturbance same as I did, but it's blind to Stanley. I see that I'm gonna have to walk him right up and push him through myself, which doesn't exactly excite me, because I don't want to get anywhere near the veil.

I go wide around Stanley and put my hand to his back. "All right, Stan. Time to go. Again." He shambles forward with my hand at his back like he's had ten too many shots at Sancho's Bar. My touch sinks partway into him, which is more than a little gross. I get unsettling flashes of his past life, pictures of his wife and his desk and his yard and a little yapping dog. It depresses me. I aim him at the veil and narrow my eyes.

"No funny business," I say.

Nothing.

I brace myself and shove Stan toward the veil. He falls through it like a rock through a black cloud. The veil doesn't rustle. Doesn't move at all. Which by now I'm finding more unsettling than when it was getting handsy. Then it pops out of sight.

Now, to figure out just what happened to my man Stan.

I open the soul map and find where I tucked Stan's soul string away. I mark it then step back into the living world and start to swipe back along the line of his life, just like I did with Karen. I backtrack a week. Before Karen met her end, before Grant found the bell. The world whips and blurs until I land in Plymouth, Virginia, once more. On the third story of a big brick corporate building, where he worked in a corner office. I recognize all of it. There's Stan, typing away at a spreadsheet but pulling every now and then at the collar of his shirt. His coloring isn't good. He keeps flicking the fingers of his left hand in and out, rubbing them. He feels constricted. His arm is going numb. Warning signs, Stan. C'mon, man... and there he goes. Mid-report. So it was a massive coronary that got him. He was alive one moment then dead the next, eyes still open, his face on his keyboard.

Enter: me. I watch myself step from the soul map and survey the scene. I take a point of pride at my response time. Less than thirty seconds.

I watch myself help Stan's soul up from his seat. He's a little disoriented, but he gets it faster than most. More than anything he's pissed off. He says he was voted most likely to work himself to death in high school, and here it actually fucking happened. "Can you believe that?" he asks me.

Sure can, Stan. Time to go.

He's still shaking his head, as if he's pissed off at his dead body, as the veil snaps him up. I watch myself look around the room for a minute then swirl open the map and step through. Job well done.

So here I am, watching the credit reel of a job I just did, which just so happens to be in a corner office with a dead, soulless body slumped over a keyboard. Nothing too out of the ordinary, but something has to happen to bring Stan back. So I wait.

I wait, and I wait, and I wait. I see the entire aftermath. The screaming secretary who stumbles across the body. The ambulance call. The medics that come in, take a pulse, and start prepping the gurney in no particular hurry. The office is in shock; they shut down early. I'm still there in a darkened room. Nothing strange yet. Nada. But somehow Stanley ended up wandering the New Mexico desert.

If it ain't happening here, maybe it's happening there.

I whip back to where I ran into Stanley in the foothills. It's still several hours before I find him, but all is quiet here, too. It occurs to me that he could have been wandering around for hours out here even before I came across him.

Who knows where he started. I spin in a circle, but see no sign of him. Nothing but cracked earth, dry, brittle bushes, and barren desert trees. Nothing on the horizon but the mountains one way and the highway with its lone light in the other. I squint at it. Kind of strange for I-85 to have a streetlight this far out in the desert. Usually it's just you and your headlights.

In fact, the light looks way too green to be a streetlight. It's almost turquoise, actually. Like the crow totems...

I start walking toward it. Then I start running, which I don't need to do, since I'm still in replay mode, but I'm running nonetheless. Because I know this ain't gonna be good.

Sure enough, the "streetlight" isn't a streetlight at all. I'm deeper in the desert than I thought. The light is coming from the desert itself, pulsing with the time of a heartbeat. It's leaking from the mouth of a spillover that looks to have serviced a river system long gone dry.

I walk into the riverbed following the light, taking the subtle bends and turns slowly, until I stop at the mouth of a cave, where the light is strong. Ancient marks surround the opening. Marks I recognize as crows, some drawn with fingers and some chipped into the rock itself. Two large boulders look like they once guarded the entrance, but they've been pushed aside, the earth ripped beneath them. The mouth has been exposed for what I feel must be the first time in generations. The turquoise light pulses in low, measured time like the heartbeat of the earth. I run my hands over the rough cave paintings as I walk inside, and their paint takes on a turquoise sheen. I have a sudden flashback to crawling through the open mouth of the hogan when Gam performed my Evilway ceremony. This is like that. I feel like I am entering a sacred, delicate place. I pull my hand from the walls, afraid, even in this echo of events, that I'll kill something special just by intruding here. I feel strongly that nobody should be here. Ever.

But somebody is. I can hear a distant squealing sound, like nails on a chalkboard. I walk toward the sound, and every inch of me is on edge, even though I know that nothing can hurt me. But old habits die hard. It's the sound that's doing it. It's a scream. I can hear it more clearly with every step. Someone is being tortured.

I'm deep in the cave now. The only color is turquoise. It's like I'm walking through the middle of a crow totem that is being destroyed. The sound is too much, so I run toward it, if only to get it over with. To see what I came here to see and be done with it.

I follow the guts of the cave around a final bend, and it opens up into a low cavern. I skid to a halt on grainy rock. In front of me, Parsons and Douglas are naked, facing away from me. The white skin of their broad backs is thickly veined in black, and their hair is slicked with sweat. They are hacking at a vein of beautiful turquoise that feathers through the earth and widens just at their feet. It is the source of the light, so powerful now that it's nearly blinding. Perhaps it *is* blinding, to them. Perhaps it is what has turned their eyes black. This one vein pulses enough light to travel through the cave and sift over the riverbed, where it's still strong enough that I mistook it for a streetlight.

It's also screaming. With every blow the agents rain down upon it, it screams. Not like any animal or human might—not out of fear or anger—but out of pure pain. It hits me like a staggering punch to the gut, worse than any sucker punch I ever felt while I was alive. It's the ground itself screaming. This is a vein of the stuff that knits together the heart of the living world, and it's being ripped apart by the agents.

I lose it. I scream at them and run toward them, as if I could hammer away at an echo of the past. As if I could change what was written. The rational part of me knows I can't, but like I said, I'm a cusser.

"You fuckers! What are you doing? You're killing her!" I don't even know who *she* is, but I know they're killing her. I swing at their imprints. My fists pass through them. I fall to the ground against the vein and am washed in light like blood, and I feel like I'm gonna cry. But I'll be damned if I cry in front of the agents. Even in front of a picture of them. So I watch.

They're hammering at something inside the vein. Smashing away like children at a piñata. Their naked bodies are bright, and slick lines of sweat seem to trace their black veins and pool in the crooks of their skin. Their eyes are manic. They both step away at the same time, in total silence, heaving with the effort, and I see that they are each holding pure turquoise.

So this is the source of the totems. This, or something very like this. Although here the agents are taking what the earth freely gave to the Circle. I've held the totems. There is nothing of this scene about them. They are like nuggets of gold that unearth themselves and tumble down the rivers to be found. This is pure theft.

My point is proven when I get a better look at what exactly they are holding, because it sure as shit ain't a crow. Douglas holds a rough chunk of turquoise in an oiled rag. It's flat on one side, like a crude whetstone. Which makes sense because Parsons holds a knife. It's jagged and unfinished, but it's clearly a knife. The blade is maybe six inches long and roughly chipped, but it still glints sharply, just like an old arrowhead or traditional skinning knife. The hilt is turquoise too but wrapped in silver wire. Parsons holds it up above him and checks its edge. His eyes flash black when he sees it. He breaks into this horrid grin, and suddenly I know what the agents have been doing all this time when I should have been watching them like a dog. They were here, hacking away at the lifeblood of the living world. Fashioning some sort of weapon from the same material the crow totems came from.

And it all comes together for me. This was how poor Karen's soul was clipped before its time. What I do with my fingers, the agents have found a way to do with a knife. It's sloppy, it's ugly, and it's a perversion, but it works. I remember seeing the glow of the thing from beneath Parsons's jacket in the Vegas hotel room.

If I ate anything anymore, I think I'd have puked it up by now. That's how wrong it feels to see a weapon crafted from the vein in front of me. As it is, I just get this phantom nausea, which is almost worse.

I have answers, but they just lead to more questions. Why would the agents care about cutting souls? If they wanted to kill someone, they could have saved themselves a lot of time and exposure to the turquoise vein if they'd just shot them. Something tells me getting rid of a dead body wouldn't be a problem for these two. And for that matter, how did they find this place? It was walled over, left in peace for generations. They must have been told by someone. A Circle member? Did we have a traitor in our ranks? If not, then that meant someone else out there knew about this place, this pulse point to the heart of our world, and told the agents. Neither option was good.

Which brings us back to our friend Stan. This shit-show

ended up with a departed soul wandering the New Mexico desert. I want to know how.

I don't have to wait long.

Douglas is pacing around, psyching himself up for something. He flaps his arms back and forth like he's about to swim a few laps then slaps at his pecs, muttering to himself. He rolls his head around on his neck and pushes against the glittering rocks of the cavern, like he could move the cave. Naked and powder-white and crazed, he looks even more like a bulldog than before. Caged and prodded, ready to rip. Then Parsons hands him the knife. He takes it by the handle with both hands, and he raises it above his head, like he's about to drive a stake into the ground. But instead, he runs at the wall of the cavern, bellowing like a midnight train.

I scream with him as I watch him slam the knife into the rock wall, but it's not precisely in the rock; it's in the space before the rock. It's in the wall of the living world itself. Once it catches, Douglas rips down on it, practically hanging off the floor from the hilt. I can see the wall between the worlds slice open in a thin white line, like a paper cut before the blood seeps out. The knife moves about a foot downward, then it catches and sticks. Douglas screams in rage, and I smile grimly. He wanted more. They wanted to get through. I can see it in the disappointment in Parsons's face as he looks away in disgust.

Nice try, assholes. Maybe you could throw a ferret through that thing, but you ain't getting through. You're staying right here.

Douglas jerks the knife back out and hands it to Parsons, who takes it and covers it with an oiled cloth of his own. Parsons walks over to where he has laid his suit over a boulder. He carefully dresses himself, but I can tell his mind is racing. Douglas slams his fist into the rock wall of the cave a few times then puts his own suit back on, leaving blood marks on the cuffs. At the mouth of the cave, the agents pause. Parsons turns to Douglas, who still seethes.

"It was lazy and foolish to think we could get through using the knife alone," he says, his voice flat and slow. "There is only one way across to the land of the dead, and we have known it all along."

Douglas nods once.

"If the knife can cut a soul, it will serve its purpose on the other side. Let us test it, someplace where we will not be noticed. Someplace with enough chaos. Then we will redouble our efforts to find the bell."

Douglas nods again. Parsons reaches in his jacket and touches the knife then disappears in a flash. Douglas reaches in his jacket, touches the whetstone, and follows him a moment later. I know where they're going, of course. Off to Vegas, where Karen will be in the wrong place at the wrong time. Spoiler alert: the knife works.

Once again I'm left alone. I walk over to the vein they've ripped apart and try to see what damage they've done, but it's so bright it almost seems to buzz. I can't see anything but retina burn. When I blink my eyes clear again, I notice smoke drifting in from the cut Douglas made. More and more seeps through, and as it hits the air of this world it starts to change into something else. That something else is Stanley Vickers. He fumbles himself together and ends up sitting on the floor of the cave like he woke up there halfway through a ten-day bender. He gets up, completely lost. He staggers into the walls and falls on the floor and scrabbles his way toward the mouth of the cave and out.

I know how this one ends, too. Soon enough his presence will start to weigh on the soul map, and in a couple of days I'll feel it, too. I'll find Stan about a quarter mile from here, for the second time. He doesn't get very far. Poor guy.

But it's not Stan that worries me anymore. What worries me is that the agents somehow found a way to this place, and they have crafted a weapon that they intend to use in the land of the dead. I remember the way their black eyes glimmered in the hotel room, when they realized, somehow, that the bell had been found.

Parsons said there's only one way across, and he's right. It's the veil. The veil that has been rotting away as the knife was being ripped out of the earth. As the knife was being constructed, the veil was breaking down. The walls of the living world might hold up to the knife, but the veil sure as shit won't. Not now.

But Parsons knows as well as I do that he can't see the veil. Even if he's prepared to slice it open, he won't find it. As far as I know, the only way you can see the veil is if you're dead, or if you're me.

So that's it then. The puzzle is snapping together. The agents are gonna take the bell, then take my job, then take the knife across the veil, and by the time they do whatever evil shit they plan on doing over there, I'll be too dead to care.

9

CAROLINE ADAMS

The crows have led us to Midland, Texas. I guess Paris will have to wait.

It's probably for the best. I'm not really the Paris type. I've seen too much weirdness to sit and smoke at sidewalk cafes and get in touch with my artistic side. Someone who sees colored smoke coming off people might be a little too in touch with her artistic side as it is. Plus there's only so much espresso I can drink before my hands start to shake. And smoking kills you. Don't even get me started on that.

I chase the bell now. I deal with the thin space between the land of the living and the land of the dead. And I'm not bummed about it, either. When the chaos things tried to latch on to me and drag me into oblivion off the highway, sure, I had a moment where I thought maybe Paris might have been a better choice. How about you take a walk down the street and then have a surprise chaos hand rip through the fabric of the air and go after your jugular? You'd be doubting your direction in life as well. But once we got on the road and the highway was sliding under us and the summer sun was shining through the window of the RV onto the front seat, I started feeling better. I love road trips. When I was a kid and couldn't sleep, Mom used to put me in the back seat of our old station wagon and drive around the neighborhood until I conked out. It still works.

Cruising aside, it's really Owen who calms me down. Warms me up. Helps bring me back. And he does it just by driving and giving me time. Although it helps that I can see the worry coming off of him in waves. He wants badly to comfort me. To reach out and touch me and reassure himself that I'm thawing out. There's another color on him, too. I've seen it in others, and it's different for each person. For Owen it's a rich cream, like foamed milk or melted white chocolate. It started to tinge his smoke when he took that bullet for me back at ABQ General Hospital, when he decided he'd rather I be around than him.

There's another word for that smoke. A four-letter word. But I don't even want to go down that road because that's just crazy, and it kind of breaks my heart to know Owen feels that way without him saying anything. It seems like a thing I shouldn't know before he wants me to know. It's a thing that's partly made real by speaking it. So until that happens, I try not to think about what his feelings mean for us. I also try not to think about how I'd answer him if he said it—and how my answer might disappoint him. Or worse, how my answer might snuff out that beautiful color of smoke. Because the truth is, right now I'm not in a position to love anyone back. I can't keep my own head on straight, much less bring someone else on board in the front seat of my life.

And now I'm starting to freak out again just sitting here. I'd say I'm seventy-five percent convinced that I'm not a complete freak of nature because of the things I see in people. That last twenty-five percent is still on the fence, though. And sometimes when I start to think too hard about it, my life gets thrown all out of whack and I wonder what the hell I'm doing with myself in an RV with a guy I like— and maybe *more* than like but maybe not—but definitely *need*. And a magic crow in my pocket. And a special bell in my sights.

Just lock me up and throw away the key. I wouldn't blame you.

I force myself to look out of the window at the desert floating by out on the horizon, and I feel a little better. I look over at Owen, and I feel even better still. I give a little fist pump. See? Old Caroline would have been paralyzed by these thoughts, her eyes open like some shocked baby who'd just tasted her first lemon, except that it would last all day and night and sometimes roll into the next day and affect every aspect of her life. Now at least I'm keeping my neurosis contained. That deserves a fist pump.

Sometimes I think if I could just make Owen realize how weird I am it might make him think twice about me. Pull over the boat and usher me out. But what I call weird, Owen thinks is special and unique. Which is true. But it's also weird. He's nice-guy understanding about it when sometimes what I need most is for someone to call a spade a spade.

We hit the outskirts of Midland, and now all of a sudden it's stop and go. Then we find ourselves in a long line of semi-trucks, and we hit full-blown stop for thirty seconds at a time. I'm not sure who lives here, but I'm willing to bet it's not the type of people I see getting in and out of these trucks and walking around with huge packs on their backs. We idle next to a supermarket, and I see a big line of conversion vans in the back of the parking lot that look set up for the long haul. A couple of two-seater cars are even set up with chairs around them that don't look like they're going anywhere anytime soon.

"What's with all the people?" I ask.

"We're in the middle of oil country," Owen says. "I suspect these are people looking for temp work on the rigs, trying to cash in on the boom."

I try to think of the kind of life someone has to have to give it all up, head to Midland, and camp out in their car in a parking lot in the hopes of finding a temp job. It makes me feel like a complete bitch for freaking out about crossing the country in this boat of an RV with my own bed and a flat-screen TV and an endless supply of gossip rags. And Owen by my side.

"It's kind of hard to follow the crows when the crows are everywhere. And they're acting very un-crow-like," I say, leaning over to look up and out of the windshield. The crows seem as confused about what they're doing here as we are. They're floating this way and that like ribbons in the breeze or hopping from tree to tree in mass movements of black. We're not the only ones taking notice, either. Stuck in standstill traffic, people are getting out of their cars and filming with their phones.

"This is as far as I think we're going to get for a bit. No sense in sitting in traffic for the sake of it," Owen says and turns off the road into the supermarket parking lot. He parks the RV in the far corner in the last free spot tailored for it. He kills the engine and sits back in his seat then looks over at me. I'm expecting a *what now*? What I get is "I think we have to move on instinct. If Joey Flatwood and Big Hill are right, the crow totems will lead us to the Keeper and the bell. Are you ready?"

I smile. There's the Doctor Bennet I remember from

ABQ General and Chaco Medical Clinic. Maybe something about the attack in the thin place steeled him. Like he saw what he was up against, saw it hurt me, and it pissed him off.

"It's like a crow convention out there," I say. "The agents aren't stupid. If we followed the crows here, they can't be far away."

Owen nods stoically. "We better move our asses then," he says. I think about asking him exactly what he thinks the two of us can do to protect the Keeper—which the rest of the Circle apparently thinks Ben hand-picked us to do— when we can barely take two steps in the thin world without getting jumped. But I think that last line of his was sort of his action-movie exit, which is cute. So I let it go. Regardless, we're on a path, and that path has led us here. No point stopping now.

We start to walk east, leaving the long line of trucks behind. It's getting into the late afternoon; the sun is at our backs, but it's still sticky hot. The streetlights are flickering on one by one. Several crows sit atop each and watch us as we walk.

SOON WE'RE WALKING through the middle of the city. I take off my long-sleeved shirt and tie it around my waist. It's still hot even in a tank top. Owen looks like he's regretting his "forever in a button-down" policy. He looks sunburned, which you'd think would be impossible given that we stepped out of the RV at six p.m., but it's true.

"You feeling anything?" he asks.

"I dunno. Would I know it if I did?"

He shrugs and dabs at his forehead with the underside of his sleeve. "Maybe it's working already. Maybe it's been working this whole time. I should have brought water." He pauses, and we lean against the still-warm brick of an office building. I can see that he doesn't have a lot of faith in wandering around waiting for feelings, and I also see annoyance, probably because he knows that I know that he doesn't have a lot of faith. He looks at me sideways.

"You know that thing you're doing? Where you know everything about me? Can you turn it off?"

I look down, and my face reddens. "I'm sorry, Owen. Sometimes I wish I could." That's a lie. I love knowing things about people. So sue me. And when I look back up at him, I know he sees through me. He's sporting the *yeah, right*, cocked-eye look.

"It's okay," he says. "If I could know how you really feel about things, I'd be all over it." His smile ticks up one corner of his mouth.

"I know it sort of... puts you at a serious disadvantage in this whole"—I pass my hand between us—"this *thing* we've got going on here."

Owen lets out a breath. "Yeah. It's quite a *thing* we've got. Just awesome. You read me like a book, and I get to take it."

"I'm a mess," I say. "You, you're ordered. It's clear as day with you. If you could see what my smoke looks like... It's a cat's cradle with a million different colors of string. I'm all over the place."

It looks like this isn't what Owen wants to hear. In fact, he kind of looks like I'm pissing him off. Which is why it's good when a stream of crows thumps its way around the corner—the heavy flapping of their wings feels like it stirs the air around me. They're flying low, by the windows, and they look like they know what they're doing. So we run after them.

We run with the crows above us as long as we can, cutting across streets and whipping around corners. We run until my lungs burn, and then we run some more. I'm sweating like a pig. I taste salt. My eyes sting. And still we run. If I ever had my bearings to begin with, I'm totally lost now. Eventually we just can't keep up with the flock. The last one passes overhead, and Owen staggers to a halt. I've got serious sweavage, and my thighs are sticking together. I double over and put my hands on my knees to catch my breath. Owen does the same. After a minute, when I feel like I can talk again, I stand. The air doesn't move here. It's like we're in a bubble. If I could, I'd strip down. I look over at Owen and see that he's allowed himself to unbutton the top button on his shirt. I laugh. It's ridiculous. He's ridiculous. I kind of love it. He looks at me and laughs, too, which means I must look much more like a farm animal than I think. Then we both look for more crows.

They're circling high over a subdivision of small houses, most of them not much bigger than a double-wide trailer. They're flat and low but well kept and brightly lit. Most have dirt front yards, but some have that crazy, thick super grass out front that can live in this type of climate. My crow totem stirs, like when you have your phone in your pocket and it phantom buzzes on you.

"The bell is close," I say. "I think it may be in that group of houses somewhere."

Owen nods. I know he can feel it too. We take a step toward the neighborhood and then freeze at the same time. Something else is here. Something close that shouldn't be. It feels like a vague muscle cramp you can't quite rub away. The crow totems are rebelling against it like opposite ends of a magnet. Whatever is coming, it's like an anti-totem.

"We gotta move," I say, but Owen is already one step ahead of me.

10

GRANT ROMER

Pap moves his sitting chair into my room so I can sleep. The last thing I remember is hearing the rustling of the newspaper and the tinkling of the ice in his drink as he takes a sip, then I'm so tired that I just nod off.

I have this dream that I'm back at the graveyard by the floating pond. The 'thin place' is what Pap called it. Everything is still strewn about, and the light is all weird and off, like an old movie. There's nobody else there, just like at the real Fairview Cemetery. Pap said other people can't see the thin places like I can, but they can feel them. And if things ain't right with a thin place, it sort of bleeds over into the people around it, and sometimes they get up and go. In my dream, things ain't right. In fact, *things* are coming out of the thin place, smoky black things that are inching toward me and molding together into arms and hands. I turn around to run, and standing right there are the bone-white men with black eyes. They smile with their yellow teeth and grab at my chest where the bell is. It burns so bad that I bolt upright in bed and cry out.

Pap is by my side in a second. "It's all right, son. It's all right. I'm right here. Just a dream."

I clutch at my chest and nearly collapse back into bed. I feel the bell still there, and I'm relieved the dream things didn't get it. You're probably thinking that would be impossible, but you wouldn't be so sure if you'd felt how hot the bell is in my hand. That's when Chaco taps on the glass. And it's not a *how you doing?* tap. It's a quick, rapid-fire tap that I already know means we got trouble. I throw open the window.

I say, "The bone men—"

"They're almost here," Chaco says. "They're both phasing again. I don't know how. They must have found another way." He's puffing in and out really fast now, talking to himself and to me. I turn to Pap to translate, but one look from me and he seems to get it.

"Can we fight them?" Pap asks, balling his huge hands into rough fists. Chaco shakes his head in a blur. "They're much faster now than they ever were, and stronger. They let the thin place possess them. They're hardly even a part of the living world now. Our only chance is to run."

I turn to Pap. "We can't fight them," I whisper.

"Then we run." Pap says to Chaco, "Meet you round back." He grabs my hand, and together we cut through the house and through the back door. We don't even close it. We run over the lawn and through the back gate, and then we're running down the alleyway between all the houses before I even really wake up completely. I'm still in my PJs, even. I look above us and see Chaco like a dark drop of oil on the black sky.

"Where we goin'?" I ask.

"Camp," Pap says. "I figure if these guys are as bad as I think they are, only thing we can do is distract them and maybe lose them. Ain't nothin' more full of distractions than that damn camp."

Pap never liked the man camp. He told me once it was full of the new kind of field worker. He called them "cocky drunks who think they're oilmen." I remember it because Pap hardly says a bad word about anyone.

"They can't take my bell, Pap," I say. "Not the bone men, not the cocky drunks who think they're oilmen, not nobody. It's a really important bell." I clutch it in one hand as I run. I speak in whispers and pull up my pajama pants. I feel like a burglar in the night.

"I know. I don't know how, or why, but I get the same feeling from it that you do. That thing is more important than me, might even be as important as you. And you're about the most important thing in the world." Pap is wheezing a bit, and I try to slow up so that he can catch his breath, but he just pulls me along faster. My heart is jack-hammering in my ears. I'm trying to listen for that *whoosh, pop* that the bone men made when they first came after me, but now I imagine that I hear it everywhere. One thing's for sure: we're being followed. I feel it even before Chaco's shrieking *caw* tips us off.

I clear my throat. "There's somebody back there."

Pap nods. "It's two of them, I think. Too dark to make out for sure. C'mon now, this way."

Pap knows this area even better than me. We run in silence this way and that, cutting through neighborhoods and over flat plots of dirt, and we only slow just as we get to the edge of town. We cross the last paved road before the man camp breathing hard and trying to look like we didn't just run a mile. I try to find Chaco ahead, but my heart is pounding too hard, and my eyeballs feel like they're shaking. I can't see him above me, but I know he's there, somewhere. A lot of men are stoop-sittin' outside of their sheds. They eye us as they smoke or drink, and almost all of them stop whatever they were doing to look our way. A couple of big guys who look drunk stumble to their feet. I don't know if they think they recognize us or what, but one calls after us. Pap pulls me along faster again. He looks left and right and then decides left, trotting now and muttering to himself, "Stupid, stupid, stupid idea."

"It's not stupid, Pap," I say. "Maybe if there are a ton of scary things around us at once, they'll all just holler 'n' go after each other and leave us alone."

Pap smiles even though I know he's scared, too. He stops to look down at me. "Now that right there, some might say is life in a nutshell." He ruffles my hair. And that's when someone grabs me from behind, and I go from feeling a little better to screaming in one second.

Chaco swoops down and flaps his wings, and the air around us seems to swim in black. "Whoa, whoa! Grant, it's all right! It's all right, my man! These are the people I told you about! They're cool!"

Chaco perches on my head, and I sag a little with his weight and stare at the two people who came out of the shadows. One is a tall, thin guy with red hair who looks like a schoolteacher, and the other is a lady with soft eyes and a nice-looking face who is holding her hair up off her neck and fanning herself with her hand. They both stare at Chaco, but they don't look surprised that a huge bird is on my head. I think they've seen him before. Pap is balling his fists, but I put a hand on his and hold it like he held mine back at home in my small space.

"My bird Chaco knows you," I say. They nod. "He says you're good people."

The lady nods. The man shrugs. "Comparatively, for sure," he says. The lady elbows him.

"My name is Caroline. This is Owen. Are you... do you have the bell?" she asks, dropping her voice, although from the way she's looking at me, I think she already knows I do. I think she knows that and a lot more about me. Still, I clutch at the bell. Chaco titters on my head.

"It's all good, man. All good. They're with us," he says.

I look back to them and nod. The lady smiles at me, and her smile makes me feel warm. The man crouches down and cocks his head at me, then he laughs. "Incredible," he says. "It's... it's ludicrous, but also it's inspired. A child. It's perfect. You're perfect."

I don't know whether to snap at the guy or blush, but Pap saves me the trouble. "We better keep moving."

He starts to press at my back to move again when we hear another scream. At first the new guys look at me like I did it, but I was just surprised that first time. I hardly ever scream. Chaco knows it wasn't me. He snaps his arrowed head to the right, back the way we came. That was a grown-man scream, which is a thing you hardly ever hear, and that sounds terrible.

"Remember how you talked about running trouble into trouble and hoping it doesn't notice you?" Chaco asks. I nod, and he bobs along. "There's a rough crowd hanging out at this makeshift booze hut. They're fixing for something. Follow me." Chaco lifts up off my head in big swoops. I turn to Pap.

"Let's follow him." I think he hears that my voice is kind of soft, because he thumps my back and pulls together a small smile for me. I straighten up.

"All right then," Pap says. The new guys nod. We all take off after Chaco.

We stand out in this place like four sore thumbs, and everyone outside of this shop Chaco takes us to knows it. I'm expecting a restaurant or something like the Roadhouse where Pap sometimes used to go with Dad. It's not like the Roadhouse. The Roadhouse has a bright sign with some letters missing on it so it reads *Radhus*. This place has no sign. It's not really a place, either. It's the same type of cheap-looking shack as every other building here; this one just has the door wide open and cigarette smoke pouring out of it and a big crowd milling around on the dirt outside getting into each other's faces. Not fighting, exactly, but fixin' to. Until they see us, that is. Then they pour it on us.

"Look at this fuckin' guy," someone yells, and I don't know who they're talking about exactly, but I think it's probably Owen. I think I like Owen, but even I know he stands out the most. He'd stand out in downtown Midland. Then I hear another person say, "Hey sweetheart, what's he pay to fuck you? I'll double it." Which I don't really follow, but I know ain't what you're supposed to say to people.

Owen surprises me by stepping forward and saying, "Keep drinking, you fat-ass. It's either going to be diabetes or cirrhosis that gets you. Then you'll be praying to God that people like her can save your pathetic life."

I don't really get what Owen's talking about, but that's okay 'cause I can tell these men don't either and they've got about twenty years on me. The fat guy shoves a few people out of the way and steps forward.

"The fuck you just say to me, boy?" he says, stomping forward. This time I expect Owen to turn tail for sure, but still he doesn't back down. Chaco lands heavily on the flat roof of the place. He squawks loudly, and I can see he's looking from the crowd here down the mud pathway back toward the entrance, where I hear another scream.

Then a *whoosh, pop*.

Pap hears it too, and even though he ain't never had the *whoosh, pop* happen to him before, he squeezes my shoulder even tighter and tries to move me behind him.

Caroline hears it and steps up between Owen and the big man before he can get to him.

"You men are gonna die here tonight if you don't start running," she says. "Fair warning."

Whoosh, pop. Closer this time. The men laugh. One spits a stream of tobacco juice at her feet, and it dangles in his beard and on his shirt, which is crossed with dark lines of the stuff. "Only ones in trouble tonight are you and your boyfriend. The old man and the kid can fuck off if they know what's good for them."

Caroline doesn't look mad, but she is looking. She's looking at this guy the way she looked at me, as if she can see more of him than anyone else on earth. Only this time she doesn't like what she sees, and it makes her sad.

"That's what I thought," she says, almost whispering.

"You first, ginger," the big guy says, and he swings a big ol' punch at Owen, wide as a house. Only when it's supposed to hit Owen, it doesn't. It hits nothing. Owen's gone. The big guy just about chucks himself over. Then there's Owen, in a blink, standing behind the guy, and he looks as surprised as anyone that he's there. Then he breaks out into this huge grin.

"Caroline, I did it! Did you see that? It's less of a step, you know? More of a pivot sort of thing and you aren't so far away when you..." He trails off when he seems to remember what he's doing there, and he lays a big heel into the fat guy's butt right as he's trying to stand. The guy goes down hard right on his chin.

"Owen, behind you!" Caroline yells and runs toward

him, but it's too late. A bottle zips through the air and clocks him right in the back of the head, and now it's Owen that's staggering. Then he's on the ground, and there's a pile-on. Caroline tries to pull them off him, but she gets wrapped up herself by another man. I want to go to them and help, even though I know I stand no chance of doing anything worthwhile, but Pap holds me back. I was really starting to like these guys, and here they are going down in a cloud of screaming and sweat and dirt and the smell of dirty metal and dog crap. We get shoved away, pushed to the outside, and I look up at Pap to tell him to let me go, but he's looking past the pile. Down the mud road. At the bone men.

Both of them are there, like powder wearing a suit and tie. There's a *whoosh, pop* and they're gone, but now it's me who's pushing Pap to get away. I can't even get out the word *run* before both bone men are in the mess of people in front of us. The tall one cocks his head, and I'm reminded of this one time when I watched a lizard for a whole hour. Just watched it look at things. That's how he looks at each man he picks up. Then he tosses them a good twenty feet with a flick.

"Where is the child?" he asks.

Another roughneck grabs at the bone man but screams as soon as he touches him and lets go like he's been burned. Pap pushes me behind him.

"Where is the bell?" he screams again, and his voice sounds so jagged and harsh that it even pauses the brawl. The tall one stares at the pile. He thinks I'm underneath, like maybe the bell is what everyone here is fightin' for. He nods at the short one, the one built like a brick wall, and this one steps forward. I almost give up the ghost by screaming when I see him. He's the one who went after me, and he's the one Chaco ripped up. His face has two huge gashes running down it, from his forehead all the way down to his chin, and they go through his eyes, which are like bleeding black marbles. He squats down and shoves his arms underneath the pile like a tractor, then in one lift he flips four or five people up and spinning in the air. They scream until they land in clumps with a sound like smashed tomatoes. He does it again. More people fly. Then there's Caroline. Her clothes are ripped up, and she's crying. The guy holding her drops everything and runs, and she falls to the ground and crawls over to Owen, who ain't moving. He's sort of crumpled, his arms and legs at weird angles and his face mushed and puffy. When the tall one sees him, his eyes flash.

"You two. I know you two. We must be close," I hear him say, even over all the running and all the fighting that's still going on at the fringes and pouring out of the smoky door to the makeshift restaurant. The tall one moves toward Caroline, who starts to back away but then stops herself. She stands tall, slowly, but she does it. Then she walks over to Owen and stands over him, inches from the tall one. She doesn't say anything. She's looking the bone man up and down.

"I can see what you were," she says. "But you aren't that man anymore."

"Less and less. Soon I will leave humanity behind altogether," he says. "The child is here. The bell is with him. We know it. Perhaps all he needs is to be drawn out." He grabs her by the arm with one hand, and with the other he reaches inside his jacket pocket. He pulls out a knife that seems to burn the air and that stains them both a weird green color. I don't need to know what type of knife it is to know that it's just *wrong*. I know in my heart that I can't let that thing touch anyone.

I scream again. "No!"

I can't even take another breath before the bulldog bone man is in front of me. This close, the *whoosh, pop* shakes my ears. His cut-up face is inches from me. His slashed eyes don't move, but I know they see me. He takes a deep sniff and looks down at my chest. Then, faster than a blink, he grabs the bell and rips it through my shirt and off my neck. The force yanks me down, and I'm on my knees. I see the other one walk up to me. His shoes stop at my hands.

"I knew you'd betray yourself, child," he says. "Compassion is a uniquely human failing. You cling to the belief that there is a way that things should be, but that is wrong. That implies order." He lifts me standing by the nape of my shirt. "You can't be blamed for thinking thus. Even we did, once. The thin place burns what is human away from you bit by bit and shows you the true nature of things."

"Go," I say. I think it comes out as a groan. I think I'm trying to say *go away*, but his grip is so cold that it burns. Everything burns. The green knife burns. The place where the bell rested near my heart burns. The bell wants to come back to me, but the short bone man grips it with his whole fist. It has no chance of escape.

"Oh, we will go. But first we need a death. That is the way of the bell." Everything becomes green as he raises the knife above me. But Pap is there. He screams and throws himself at the arm holding the knife, but it's not enough. I barely feel the bone man move. He keeps raising the knife over my head until Chaco hits him like a cannonball. He staggers backward, one hand protecting his face as Chaco rips at the knife, but as soon as he touches it, he screeches and shrinks away like he's been stung bad, which gives the bone man an opening. He snatches Chaco around the neck and slams him to the ground. Chaco twitches and flops then goes still.

"Chaco!" I scream. "That's my best friend! What did you do to my best friend?"

The bone man doesn't care. Why would he? I bet he never had a best friend in his life. He grabs me by the neck and brings the knife up again. Pap is scrabbling, and I'm pulling against him, but we're not moving a muscle on the bone man, until Pap spits in his face. He spits right in his eyes. That catches him up.

"Leave him be!" Pap yells. "You're perversions. Both of you. You ain't fit to touch my grandson."

The tall one turns to him, and that lizard-like interest comes back. He blinks the spit away, which is the first time I think I've seen him blink. He drops me.

"One death is as good as another," he says. Then he plunges the knife into Pap's stomach, and Pap drops to the ground before I can even scream. His eyes are open, but there's nothing behind them.

Even though I can't hold it, I feel the bell start to pull itself together. Chaco lets loose a heartbreaking cry, and I feel him rushing toward me. I watch the black eyes of the bone men widen as the glow of the silver grows, and grows, and grows.

"Ring it," the tall one says.

The bell is rung. It sounds like a shotgun, and it sounds like a whisper, but mostly it just sounds sad.

11

THE WALKER

I am there.

I am there when the agents come to Midland. I walk behind them as they reach the camp. I reach for Caroline as she is swallowed up in the brawl, but my hands swipe nothing. I scream for Chaco to help, but he says that his charge is Grant. He says it again and again like he has to constantly remind himself or he'd be diving in.

And when the bell is ripped from Grant and Chaco does dive in, I see him dashed to the floor. I scream when Parsons plunges the turquoise knife into Grant's grandfather. I watch as it cuts a soul that is still strong, that still had time. I watch as the knife destroys the natural order of things and rewrites a small portion of the soul map in one jagged, muddy swipe. My world lurches. I get a sense of drunken vertigo, and everything leers to one side for a second before righting itself again. I can do nothing. I am worthless.

Now all Parsons or Douglas needs to do is stab himself and ring the bell. Then I hand over the keys to the car and cross over forever, and one of them takes my place. I close my eyes. In a way, I want it to happen. In a way, it's bitter-sweet. I wish I could tell Caroline goodbye, but my life has never been on point in the timing department anyway. It makes sense that it would end like this. Like I got hung up on.

Parsons says, "Ring the bell." I squeeze my eyes shut. I hear the bell chime like a hammer striking a brass pipe that's as big as a car...

...And nothing happens to me.

I open my eyes and find both agents very much alive and the bell very much rung. The sound's shockwave has formed a bubble around the agents that is distorting time. I remember it well from when I died and rang the bell. The shockwave pushes outward slowly, like a kid blowing a bubble. But that was when I was in the thick of it. It never occurred to me that someone might ring the bell in the presence of death and not actually be dying themselves. But now that it's happening, I remember Caroline and her last moments with Gam. The bell formed then, but Gam told her not to ring it. She could have, but she didn't. The agents just did. And now the agents are waiting inside their bubble of time. They can only be waiting for one thing.

I feel the tug of the soul map calling me to a man named Abernathy Romer, but I don't need the hint, because I'm already there. I watch as the soul of Abernathy sits up from his dead body and turns to his grandson, who is huddled over him. He reaches for Grant, and his hand passes right through the kid. He knows in that second that he's been cut from his grandson, and he weeps. It's a soft, hitching sound that is all the more heartbreaking for the fact that I know from his soul string that he's only cried twice in his adult life: once when his grandson was born and once at the death of his son and daughter-in-law. He calls their names first.

"James? Becca?"

He gets no answer. He stands and watches Grant slump over him, shaking with silent tears. "So I am alone, then," he says.

"No, sir," I say.

He flips around and puts his hands up, eyes wide.

"No more fighting, Ab. All we can do now is watch and wait." I point at the agents in the bubble of the bell and add acidly, "Like them." I don't know if they can see us, too, but they aren't on the lookout for us anyway. They're on the lookout for the veil. They watch with fierce intensity, scanning the horizon like stranded sailors looking for rescue.

Ab's hands lower slowly. His eyes stay wide. "Are you..." He trails off. I nod. I want to sit down with him over a beer. I want to shoot the shit. I want to tell him how he was robbed of years he should have had with Grant. But the veil is here. Funny how even outside of time, there's never enough time.

"What in God's name is that thing?" Ab asks.

"That's what everyone's waiting for." The veil sweeps down the dry, cracked mud street of the camp with all the presence of a strip of iron, and when it enters the bubble of the bell, the agents see it, along with everyone else.

It's sort of like if a big stage prop falls down in the play that is our living world, and all the people working behind the scenes in black are suddenly bang on in the spotlight. Everyone's focus meets at once, and everything within the bubble is revealed. The agents see me. Grant sees his grandfather's soul standing over him. Owen sees us both. I see Caroline.

Caroline sees me.

My name is on her lips. I can see it. And I see something

else, too. Something I haven't seen for a long time. I see someone who misses me. I can't tell you what that feels like after what seems like an eternity of people terrified to see me. Here's a woman who misses Ben Dejooli. Not the Walker. Just Ben. She doesn't cry out or yell or run to me. She just smiles through her tears. Until the agents step between us.

"Benjamin Dejooli," Parsons says slowly, splitting into a yellow smile. "Remember us?"

"You screwed up, Parsons. If you wanted my job, you had to off yourself and ring the bell at the same time. You two are such fanboys that I'd have thought you'd have picked up on that by now."

Douglas laughs. It's a disturbing, hyena laugh. Quick and clipped. "We don't care about your job anymore, Ben," Douglas says.

Parsons nods slowly in agreement. "You see, you're the ferryman. Nothing more than a glorified day laborer. You hold every soul by the hand and escort them to the threshold like you were their arm candy. You are doomed to this for eternity. Giving everything, getting nothing. Why in this world or the next would I want that?"

I consider myself pretty quick on the draw when it comes to swapping barbs, but shit, this one floors me. I was just starting to feel good about my job.

"You have no idea what I do," I say. "You can't. If you walked the soul map, it would destroy you."

"We don't come to walk the soul map, Mr. Dejooli. We come to own the map on which you walk," Parsons says. "Your peasant's day job doesn't concern me. I know what you do. I also know what you can't do. You can't cross the threshold. You take the souls to the veil, never beyond."

"The veil is closed to the living. Those are the rules."

"Those *were* the rules." Parsons's black eyes are like pits of coal in his face.

He trades Douglas the knife for the bell. Douglas positions the knife in his hand with the care of a boxer wrapping tape. Then he eyes the veil just as he did the wall back at the cave. He has an audience this time: Caroline, Owen, and Grant, along with the soul of Abernathy. Anyone from the camp in the land of the living who is paying attention is seeing what they can't possibly understand, and many are struck dumb in the middle of the brawl.

Of all of them, Grant is the worst to see. With one hand he clutches at his heart, where his bell was ripped from him. With the other hand he reaches for a living picture of his grandfather only feet from him but beyond his grasp. It's not fair that he should have to see this. None of it is fair. But it's the way it is.

Douglas runs at the veil the way a bear sprints, his body seemingly falling over itself. He screams like a demon and then jumps with the knife high above his head. He brings it down on the veil, and it sticks. He uses his body to drag it down, and down, and down. He falls to the ground with the knife in his hand, laughing like a maniac, because he's ripped it right open.

There's a loss of pressure so great that it brings every living thing near the bubble to their knees. Only Ab and I are standing. Even the agents are buckled over, but they recover. They grit through it and stand tall and suck in the pain that must be pummeling them. I realize that this is what they've been training for. This is their moment. Parsons screams in triumph and holds his hands out wide.

"Do you see, Benjamin? Do you see? Nothing can keep us from him now!" Parsons screams.

Him? I don't like the sound of that, but I don't have a lot of time to think about it. I'm scared shitless. I admit that freely. I'm looking around this place like I stepped into a bad party and all I want to do is turn around before the guys with guns realize I'm there. And I may have done just that—swirled open the map, walked through, taken a stroll over to Cancun for a couple of personal days to piece all of this together—if it weren't for Caroline. Caroline is on the ground with her hands pressed against her ears. I want to run to her and envelop her, but I know I can't. I want to tackle the agents, but I know I can't. Still, I feel I owe it to everybody to watch. So I watch. That's me. Fuck the Walker; they should just call me the Watcher.

But you know who doesn't just stand around feeling sorry for himself? Abernathy Romer. He's been seething at Parsons the whole time. When Parsons holds his hands out, palms open, swimming in victory, Ab swats the bell out of his hand.

While the bell rings, it exists on every plane, but Ab doesn't know that. Ab doesn't care. He sees something that is precious to his grandson, stolen from him, and he wants to give it back. His hand passes right through Parsons, but it connects with the ringing bell. It's out and spinning in space before anyone knows what happens.

Scratch that. I should say "before anyone but Grant knows what happens."

Grant sees it all. He's on top of it. He's so quick on the draw that he scampers out and snatches it mid-air like one last handshake from his grandfather. He clutches it to his chest, and the kid smiles. Finally, he smiles. When Ab nods at him in approval, he smiles wider.

Parsons looks at his empty hand, confused. Douglas pushes him toward the split veil. "Let's go!" Douglas says. "Forget the bell! We don't need it anymore!"

As broken as it is, the veil is already slowly oozing together again. The hole the agents cut is closing, just like it did back in the cave. They don't have enough time to go for both the bell and the veil. Parsons turns to Grant, and the look he gives would probably kill a normal kid, but Grant isn't a normal kid. Grant squares his shoulders.

"Go!" Douglas screams again. It seems like it takes an effort of will from him, but he rips his gaze from the bell and turns to the veil. He doesn't hesitate. He runs and leaps through the crack. Douglas follows without so much as a word back toward us.

And now I've got a problem on my hands.

Whatever those powder-haired freaks want to do on the other side, I guarantee you it's not gonna be good for any of us. Not good for the living world, the dead world, or any world in between. Parsons is the brains of the duo, and he's pissed about losing the bell back to Grant, which is good, but these two are like crocodiles. They're not going away; they just keep swimming until they get what they want.

And now they're swimming around unchecked on the other side.

Ab looks at me. Grant looks at me. Owen looks at me. Caroline looks at me. All of them watch me even as the ringing—and their vision of me—begins to fade.

"Ah, shit," I say. Because I know what it might mean. When Death takes a holiday, the dead go on vacation. But I can see it in Caroline's eyes. I've got no choice. "After you," I tell Ab. He nods. He turns to Grant and clutches at his heart, then he holds his hands out. "I love you, son," he says. Even if he can't hear it, Grant gets it. He's crying silently, but he nods.

Ab walks through the veil.

I have seconds left. I take one last look at Caroline and

Owen, then I go for the rip. It's just about shoulder width. I dive for it. It catches on my waist. I push through and fall out and over like a newborn animal. And just like that, the living world and the world in between are lost to me.

I'm beyond the veil now, in the land of the dead.

12

OWEN BENNET

When Parsons stabs Grant's grandfather, I'm thinking subcutaneous perforation for sure, and probable bowel piercing. Almost certainly there will be internal bleeding. But it's in the stomach proper, not the liver, and Parsons pulls the knife out cleanly and doesn't go for more. I'm thinking that if there's a medical building in this camp, there's a good chance we can save his life. Instead the man drops dead instantly.

It's the knife. Something about that knife is an aberration. I recognize the rock it's made from, of course. I put that together as soon as Parsons took it from his jacket. It's the same as my totem. But in shaping it into a weapon, the agents created something terrible.

When the bell rings, I can see it all—the world of the Walker. Of Ben. And, of course, like a knight in shining armor, there's the man himself. If he is a man anymore. Whatever he is, it's done him good. He's standing there like he's just pushed open the doors as a late entrant into a black-tie party and he's the guy everyone's been waiting for.

Especially Caroline. I don't even need to look at her to know. But I look at her anyway. I can't tell if she's in awe or if she's scared out of her mind. All I know is that there's a connection there. A strong one. One I've never quite been able to spark between us. And I can't even be mad. I can't even blame her. This man died for his sister, took up the mantle of Death, and has been keeping the balance between life and death like some sort of dark king for the past year. Meanwhile a man has just died, and I—the doctor, mind you—am standing around blinking like a cow.

I'm seeing Grant's grandfather in two places now, so I know there's a good chance my mind has finally broken. There's his body, and then, through the hole the bell ripped into the air, I see him again. It takes me a second to realize that it's his soul. The agents and Ben are talking, but the ringing of the bell is still shaking my head. Plus my left ear feels puffy and useless from when one of the camp meatheads socked me, so I can't hear what they're saying.

Douglas, the thick one, gets a running start and lashes out with the knife at what looks like a barrier of burned paper. It splits open, and then it's like the barometer drops fifty points. I'm thinking we've lost everything. We lost a good man to the knife, we lost the bell to the agents, and now we're going to lose the agents to whatever lies beyond. Then Grant's grandfather swipes out at Parsons. There's a glinting in the air, and Grant dashes from his crouch and makes a spectacular, cross-dimensional catch. His grandfather reaches for him in farewell, but with the bell safely on our side, the rift is sealing fast. Soon they're parted. What's on that side will stay there, and the agents are on that side.

The aftermath of the opening and closing and of the ringing of the bell sits on everyone within eyeshot like an elephant. I'm the first to speak.

"Caroline," I say, and I admit it, it's partly to break her train of thought, which I'm sure is careening around Ben Dejooli Mountain. But mostly because I know that we have to pick ourselves up and dust ourselves off. The agents succeeded in something. And anything they succeed in is bound to be a mess for us. Caroline is staring at the spot where Ben disappeared. She doesn't even know I'm calling for her until I touch her shoulder.

"Caroline," I say gently. She starts. She's bleeding from the lip. I roll my cuff to a clean spot and gently dab at it. I find myself pushing a damp strand of hair back off her face. She either allows it or is too stunned by events to stop me. I'd like to assume the former, but after seeing Ben across time and space, it's most likely the latter. "The agents," I say. "We have to find them."

Caroline shakes her head. "They're gone."

I stand back and check her over. The dirt and the tears and the scrapes only serve to make her more beautiful. I'm reminded of those times when we were on shift together at ABQ General and running around from patient to patient, both of us rumpled and disheveled and tired, but fighting the same fight. Those times she'd smile at me at four in the morning as we passed in the hall. That was when I started to fall in love with her, I think.

And suddenly she's looking at me and her face is softened and she's back here, in the land of the living, with me. And I remember how she can basically read me like a book, so I shake my head as if that will clear my thoughts. I'm sure I'm as red as a fire hydrant. I touch my face. It comes away red, all right. With blood. "God, I must be a mess," I say. I try to dab at my face, but she holds my hand away and keeps it in hers.

"Let it coagulate. Just a few cuts. You'll get your shirt all bloody," she says.

As much as I want to stand here, my hand in hers, I can't shake the image of Douglas running full tilt with that horrid knife held high. "We've got to go after them."

"They're beyond us now," she says. "Beyond even the thin world. They're in the world of the dead. The world beyond." She turns to Grant, who is sitting again, slumped over, near his grandfather. He's holding the bell, but it's Chaco he's looking at. Poor Chaco, a broken mound of feathers on the cracked mud. The camp men have mostly scattered now, but I know they'll be back. I know we have to get out of here, but I'm not about to rush Grant. Without speaking, Caroline moves over to him and lowers herself down to both knees.

"I'm so sorry, Grant," Caroline says, and she's looking at him, but I know she's also looking into him. At the color of him. At his essence. She lays one hand gently on his shaking back. The other she passes lightly over him, grabbing smoke. Whatever she sees makes her eyes well with tears, but I can see her mind working. Then, out of nowhere, she says, "You weren't a burden to your grandfather. You gave him such joy. If he was ever sad, it was only because of how he wished you could have made your mom and dad as happy as you made him."

Grant's shaking subsides a little. He looks up at Caroline. "How do you know?"

"Because I saw it. How much he loved you... it came off him in waves. He blazed with it." Caroline holds out a hand to him. He takes it, and she helps him up. The three of us stand around Chaco, and the dusty wind tousles his feathers.

"He was an awesome bird..." I begin, but Grant stops me by stepping forward and kneeling down next to him.

"Chaco," he says. "I have the bell. I'm the Keeper still." He presses his little finger gently to Chaco's head, brushing the small feathers of his face. "That means we're still best friends. You told me. That means you have to get up."

I want to take the kid and hug him. I don't think I can watch him talk to his broken best friend. I think it'll rip my heart out.

The good news is I don't have to for long, because Chaco stirs.

Chaco's broken wing stretches out and snaps together again. His bulging neck straightens. His claws flex. His black eyes open, and they find Grant. Chaco twitters. Grant smiles and holds out his little arm, and Chaco flips himself up. He shakes his head like he's taken a bad fall then takes a wobbly walk up to perch on Grant's head.

The wind drops on a dime and the dust settles, but I don't get the feeling that the storm has ended, only that we're standing in the eye of it. Grant looks up at Chaco, and I think they're having some sort of silent conversation. When he looks down at us again, I can see in his eyes that my hunch is correct.

"The bone men, you call them the agents. They did a really bad thing. They ripped open the veil. It was sick to begin with because of them, but then they pretty much broke it." Grant says. "And Chaco says that if it's broken, things can come through."

"What things?" I ask. Grant and Chaco look over at me at the same time. The double weight of their gaze gives me goose bumps but not as much as what Grant says.

"Things from the other side. Things that shouldn't be here. Bad things."

Grant and Chaco look at each other again.

"What else does Chaco say?" I ask.

Grant smiles at me through all his pain and all his loss.

"He says he'd be my best friend even if I didn't have the bell."

13

THE WALKER

S o now that I'm over here on the other side, beyond the veil, I bet I know what you wanna know.

You want to know if I'm seeing God. Maybe you think I'm staring at a blazing figure sitting on a throne behind a set of gleaming pearly gates. Maybe you think that by crossing the veil I'm somehow free of my job and am getting reborn. Maybe you think what I see over here is so crazy, so awe inspiring and beyond description, that I'm struck dumb. Maybe you think I'm seeing beyond the racing edges of the universe, like I'm surfing the Big Bang.

Well, you're all wrong.

Don't feel bad about it. Hell, the Navajo don't even have what you might call a totally formed idea of what happens after we die. We're fine with the multiple worlds thing—I remember Gam used to tell Joey and me about how we humans had to go through five worlds just to get to the one we lived on, so I shouldn't fuck it up by tossing my cigarette butts on the ground. But as to what happens after we die? The Navajo don't really go in for that. In fact, my people believe that chances are after we die we sort of hang around because we're pissed off at those of us that are still living. We give the dead some things in the forms of offerings, mostly to get them to stop lingering. Best-case scenario is they disappear back into the great balance of things.

In fact, now that I think about it, and after having dealt with poor Karen and Stan 2.0, maybe the Navajo aren't so far off. No more so than anyone else. But don't worry, we didn't get it exactly right either.

What I'm staring at is a river. It's a massive, glowing river that looks like it's floating a billion flashlights. I know instantly that these are the souls I deliver. When I push them through the veil, I'm delivering them to this river. Ab and I stand on the shore just watching them. Neither of us can speak. The souls provide all the light there is in this place, but it is plenty. Everything has this mesmerizing glow about it, and for a second I forget everything, even the agents who ducked in here minutes before me. It's just Ab and me, standing side by side, following the souls, like fireflies, with our eyes.

Then Ab says, "I gotta go." It startles me.

"Yeah? Where? Into the river?" It looks kind of nice. Like swimming with a bunch of glowing fish.

"Yeah, but not just anywhere in there. I gotta go thatta way." Ab points down the right side of the riverbank.

"You act like you've been here before or something," I say, my mouth still not quite working right. "Why not that way?" I point down the left bank.

Ab shakes his head. "Nope. No way. That's not my way. My way is that way."

"You mean you can't go left?"

"I could, I suppose," Ab says. "But I don't want to." He steps forward into the river, and his feet leave no mark upon the sand. He goes into the water up to his knees then pauses. He turns back to me.

"Grant," he says. "What will happen to him?"

"I don't know. But if he's with Caroline and Owen, he's in good hands."

Ab lowers his head a bit, his brow furrowed. He takes another step in the water, and it starts to glow around him.

"I'm sorry, Ab," I blurt out. "I fucked up, man. I should have seen the knife coming. I should have followed the agents, and when I lost them, I should have known it was trouble. I let my guard down, man. I let it down and you died. That knife never should have happened." I look at my own feet. I make two heavy prints in the sand. When I look up again, Ab is smiling sadly at me.

"It's all part of the plan, young man."

"No, it's not. You don't understand. That knife, its purpose is to destroy the plan. It was created to ruin the plan. I saw your soul string, Ab. You had time left. You shouldn't be here. You should be back at home, with Grant, drinking a glass of whisky on the rocks and reading the Midland Reporter." I feel tears come to my eyes, and in a stupid act of defiance, I refuse to wipe them, as if that will make them go away. "You know, you think you know your job, and then you start feeling good about it, and that's when you fuck up. That's prime fuck-up time."

"Hey," Ab says, not harsh but enough to stop my blubbering. "I don't know much. Even after all these years living, I feel I'm going out knowing less than the day I came in. But I do know this. If I wasn't supposed to be here, I wouldn't be here."

I put my hands on my hips. I don't know how I can make him understand about the knife. I think he sees the frustration in my face because he says, "I get it, son. That knife is bad news. But I want you to consider for a second that even it has its place. Maybe breaking the plan is part of the plan."

I try to consider it. A thing that can alter the soul map, which is essentially the plan of the living world, also being a part of the plan? It's too much for me. I shake my head.

"Don't worry about it," Ab says. "You just keep going. Do me a favor. Watch out for my grandson. If you can." Ab sinks into the water up to his chest. His lower half disappears. The glow around him grows.

"I will."

"Now you go get those rat bastards that stuck me." He's up to his neck now. "They ain't supposed to be here." I nod. He smiles at me. Then he dips under, and he's gone. He's a glow now. I watch his glow spin around and then float peacefully down the river to the right. I can't help but smile myself. If I were to hazard a guess, even though I think he was a content man, I'd say Abernathy Romer hadn't smiled like that in years.

Now it's just me on the shore. Wherever Ab is going, that's not where the agents went. I turn to the left. I walk about fifty feet, scanning the ground. I see what remains of two sets of footprints, which tells me that the vein rock won't work here—there's no phasing or skipping space. The agents are hoofing it on foot. I look in their direction, but the river bends and twists and the shoreline changes terrain, following it. I can't see the men themselves, so I start running.

I get about five hundred feet down the shore before I realize that the veil isn't following me. It sits like a sad, lost dog right where I came in. Its tattered, broken silence serves as a reminder: as long as I'm over here, I'm not doing my job. This hits home harder when I look back the way I came and see that the bobbing soul lights have floated away from where I came in, and nothing else has replaced them. The water is blank. Empty. The inflow has stopped.

I pick up the pace, running full tilt now, following the footprints of the agents, which seem to fill with oily water like parking lot puddles.

The scenery begins to shift on me. No more flat beach. Soon I'm running over pebbles, then rocks, then I'm dodging around boulders. Another couple hundred feet, and the earth starts to jut up around me. Soon I'm running through a canyon that zigzags all over the place. The soul light flickers and wavers like a flashlight under water. I look to my right and see the souls down this way are acting up, zipping all over the place, sometimes surging out and taking almost human form before crashing down into the water again. I feel it too: the farther I go down this side of the river, the more chaotic everything becomes. I don't think it's the agents doing it, either. I think it's the river itself. It flows two ways. There's the way Ab went, and then there's this way. The other way.

Soon even the terrain itself can't seem to decide on a form. The inlets and breaks in the rock walls that border the river shift before my eyes. It's like I'm running through a scatterbrained formation of a river. New earth pushes up through splits in the ground then breaks down seconds later. The river cuts one way through the canyon, then in a blink it changes course and cuts another way. The walls of rock recede and expand, almost as if they're breathing. The flow is in the same direction, but at one glance it seems to go uphill, then down, then around, then through overhangs that break apart the second I pass them. I focus on putting one foot in front of the other and scan the horizon when I can.

A pillar of stone shoots into the air, missing me by an

inch, and when I stop to right myself, I see the agents up ahead. Parsons is in the lead, and Douglas lopes just behind him. Douglas carries the knife in his closed fist, tip down, hilt up, pumping it in time with his stride. Parsons carries something, too. It looks like a small book. He holds it up and runs blindly forward behind it.

I feel that this side of the river is normally a place of chaos but that the presence of the knife has really revved things into overdrive. The earth around Douglas blurs and stutters. The soul light ebbs and flows around him. The two agents look like glitches in the program out here.

Parsons comes to a skidding stop, with Douglas a few paces after. Parsons flips the book around, looking to his right at the river. This is my chance to catch them. I pick up speed.

Douglas hears me first, and he lets out this low growl that gets Parsons's attention. I don't get any patronizing smile this time—this time Parsons is pissed off. It's a minor victory, but I'll take it.

"I don't have time for you right now, Dejooli. Go back to your boat, ferryman."

"I don't give two shits what you've got time for. Clearly you've got enough time to stick the laws of the universe in a blender with that damn knife of yours. I feel like you can take a second here to explain to me what exactly it is that you're planning on doing. You know, before you really, cosmically fuck everything up. I'd ask you where the hell you're going, but judging by the way you're reading that book, I'm about ninety percent sure you don't know yourself."

Parsons, who was never a real talker to begin with, even before he went and bleached himself, doesn't even give me the time of day. He just nods at Douglas, who grins and takes a step forward. The jagged cuts that span his face seem not to bother him in the slightest. "Wait," Parsons says, and Douglas pauses. "Give me the knife. We can't risk losing it." Douglas shrugs and hands Parsons the knife, then he balls both hands into fists and walks toward me.

I smirk. I'm not worried. It's easy to feel cocky about yourself when you're already dead. I spit on the sand. "Really, Douglas? Are you that much of a dumbass? You know you can't hurt me." I hold my hands out as if I'm welcoming him. Douglas cocks one arm and throws a haymaker mid-stride that shuts me right up. It knocks me off my feet and sprawls me out along the shuddering, shifting riverbank.

"Forgot what it feels like to get hit, Dejooli?" Douglas asks. He saunters over to me and grabs me by the shirt. "The thing about this place is that there are no laws. No rules. Only form and destruction. Here, you're just another form." He pulls me up by the collar. "And I am destruction." He slams his fist across my face, and I see stars. He drops me, and I scrabble for footing. He seems to enjoy it. He revs up for a kick, but when he lashes out, I catch his foot and wrench it like a bottle cap. He howls and goes down hard on his side.

"Cuts both ways, Douglas," I say. "If you can hit, I can hit. And you don't have the strength of ten men out here. Just one. And barely that."

Douglas curls his lip and stands, limping. "I've never killed a dead man before. But I guess there's a first time for everything." He throws himself forward and uses his momentum to snatch me into a bear hug. I see it coming, but I'm not that big of a guy. Every time I got into a fight back at Chaco, all the bigger guys—which was almost all of them—would use this same approach, like they could just crush me out of existence. The first few times I ended up on the wrong side of it, it sort of did feel that way until my old partner Danny Ninepoint had to save my ass. But then I learned to use their momentum against them. I sidestep Douglas and fling him behind me like a duped bull. He falls flat on his stomach. This is my opening. I jump up in the air with my knee out, ready to crack down on his back, but just then the lay of the land switches on us. The ground rolls and cracks, and I'm caught in an upthrust of rock that slams into my knee and flattens me even as it carries me up into the air. It tumbles Douglas onto the floor like a hamster in a wheel, end over end until everything comes to rest. Except that I'm fifty feet in the air now, marooned on a square patch of rock.

Douglas slowly stands, dusting himself off. He shields his eyes and looks up at me. Then he laughs. "I hope you like the view, Dejooli!" he screams. "You may be there a while!"

I look over the edge and immediately feel sick. This is a true mesa. The sides are sheer and smooth. I always hated heights. It's in my blood. The Navajo are a plains people for a reason. It's hard to tumble to your death in miles of open grassland. I always appreciated that. Never more than right now. I do the only thing I can: I spit down at him. Like some kid leaning over a bridge. Real mature, I know. He sidesteps it easily. Then he's forced to dodge another jut of earth himself. It almost takes his legs right out from under him. All around us, the land is going haywire. Dust coats the air like mist. It's as bright as midday one second, then pitch black for a blink, then everything is in this gloaming color, then marine blue, then bright again. There's no rhyme or reason to it, but it does seem to be getting worse. When I look around, I think I can see why.

We're at the edge of things. Just beyond where Douglas limps over to Parsons, the river disappears. The horizon is a thin line of black, and beyond that is just a void, like a spot between stars. It turns my stomach a bit, so I flip around, back the way I came. I can see the river wind off beyond sight, and the world seems to settle along with it. Form, function, order. Just seeing it helps calm my racing heart. I think I'm getting a hint of what Ab meant when he said he felt that this way was best for him. I almost reach out to it. Only Parsons's triumphant laugh gives me pause. I snap around and find him holding the book out at arm's length.

"Now!" he says. "This is it! But quickly! Already it changes!"

And without a second's hesitation, he runs right into the river. Douglas takes one last look up at me. He gives me a dismissive shake of the head, the kind that says I ended up being even less of a factor than he thought I would be. Nine-point used to give me those from time to time. They burned me every single time. Then Douglas is splashing off after Parsons. The bobbing soul lights seem to vibrate as he passes. They zip out of the way of the two men then spin around them like embers caught in an updraft. The agents sink and sink, and then they're gone, just like that. I scramble to the edge of the ledge, scanning the river. Crazy or not, they're still human, both of them. I figure they gotta come up some time. But they don't. And then a minute goes by. And another. And I realize it's just me here now. Alone again. Stuck on a shifty ledge above a churning world.

14

CAROLINE ADAMS

I think I pined. I didn't mean to pine, but I think I pined when I saw Ben through that rip in the air. Which sucks, because not only am I not a piner—I pride myself on not being a piner—but that was about the worst time in the world to get starry eyed. A man had just been murdered, for crying out loud. We were in the middle of man-camp hell. Dust flying, people yelling and fighting—and a little boy screaming. It's times like that when I'm supposed to be managing the situation, but instead I got zapped by the sight of Ben. You know who managed the situation? Owen. You know who I stand to hurt the most by all this nonsense with Ben? Owen.

It's a joke, really. A cruel joke. Just when I think the guy is beyond me, he pops up. He did that for months and months in my brain. I'd be at the gas station waiting for the boat to fill up and—*bam!*—surprise Ben thoughts! We played blackjack while he took his chemo regimen with those same blue-faced cards they were selling by the cash register. Or when we got waved through a cone zone back in Louisiana and there was a cop who looked just like him, even wore his pants a little high on his hips like Ben did. I'm doing nothing but flipping through a gossip rag when I see that cop and—*bam!*—surprise Ben thoughts!

But this time it was surprise Ben. Surprise *the guy himself*. In a way it was a blessing that I only had seconds to see him, to process him. Like one last voice message from someone who is gone forever, just a few seconds long, a quick hi and goodbye. You can delete that without going too crazy over it. Any longer and I would have made even more of an ass out of myself than I did.

When I turn to Grant, my skills finally kick in, and I become the nurse I'm supposed to be. Grant's grandfather is gone. Grant's smoke is weak. He's going into a state of shock, which makes sense since he saw the soul of his grandfather pass into the great beyond. I had to go talk to my school counselor for a while because I accidentally locked myself in the basement storeroom at school when I was about his age. I thought that was bad. This kind of thing would have sent little girl Caroline right off the deep end. So I do the first thing that all nurses do when they deal with a patient in shock. I let him know I'm here in a completely nonthreatening way. I reach out and gently touch his shoulder, heaving with sobs. He looks up at me, and I can see why he is in pain. I can read it dancing on his skin, leaking from his eyes, and swirling like unformed words around his chapped lips. It has less to do with his grandfather dying than it does with how he feels like crap for dragging his grandfather down during what would be the man's final days. He accepts death in the way a child can—because he has to. What he can't accept is how his grandfather had to live after Grant's parents died. I see all of this as clear as a book, and the clarity almost staggers me.

I hold myself together because one thought cuts

through: he's wrong. Grant is wrong to think his grandfather found him a burden. I know he's wrong, because I saw his grandfather's smoke too. And I saw how it only really shone true when he was with Grant, the two of them, running along with Owen and me.

And just like that, I know how to help him. I know how to fix his color. I see his pain as gaps in his smoke, and I know how to smooth them over. I know the words. So I say them. It's like I'm smoothing over a cracked vase with fresh clay. In fact, I see it happening. My own smoke comes off of me and flows over his. Changes it. It doesn't quite bring it back to the brilliant color it was when I first saw him—he's far too sad for that shine right now—but it turns it into something close. Something that could one day get back to that color.

Grant stands. He takes my hand. It takes a lot to floor the little guy. It takes even more to floor Chaco, who literally rises from the dust in front of us and hops up onto Grant's head. I remember Ben's grandmother's bird, just like this. Probably the same one, in the way that these creatures span across time and space. It stuck with her to the end, as I held her hand. I have no doubt Chaco will be around for the end of Grant, too, and will do his best to make sure it doesn't happen anytime soon.

Chaco snaps his gaze down the dirt road, past the crowd that is slowly pooling at the edges of our group. The crow caws, and Grant scrambles around me to where he can see around the buildings at the edge of the camp and out into the desert. I follow his eyes. There's an oil rig not far out there, painted red in the sunset, but that's about it. I turn back to Grant. His eyes are unfocused, almost like he's in a trance. I think he can see more than I do, just like I see more than others do, but his talent is different.

"What's out there?" I ask.

"A thin place," Grant says. "It's where I found the bell."

Owen steps up to us, still stemming the blood on his face with his cuff, despite my fussing. "Guys, I hate to break up the party. It's been such a lovely time. Charming little camp you've got here. But the natives are getting restless again. If we don't get out of here soon, we're going to end up in another fight or in jail. And one brawl a day is plenty for me."

"Grant, we have to get you someplace safe," I say.

Chaco caws again and leaps from Grant's head with a swoop. "There's nowhere safe," Grant says, translating for us. "We're the only ones who can stop it."

He's in full-blown Keeper mode now. I recognize the look from Ben's grandmother, when she gave me the bell back at Chaco. It's an ageless look. Focused but distant.

"Stop what, buddy?" Owen asks, his voice plugged up by his swollen nose.

"That thin place is breaking," Grant says, and then he takes two running steps down the dirt road before pausing and turning around again. In a second, he switches back to the little boy he is at heart. His face softens and his brow furrows as he looks down at where his grandfather's body lies. His smoke stirs and slows and darkens, but his color stays true, even deepens a little.

"You all right, Grant?" I ask, which is a ridiculous thing to ask. Of course he's not. None of us are, in the grand scheme, but he looks up at me and nods.

"I know Pap's not there," he says, looking at the body. "That's not him. But still, it..." He pauses, swallows.

"Sucks." Owen says, taking his hand away from his face. Grant looks at him and then nods. "We're with you, Grant," Owen says. "Take us to where we need to be." Owen's eyes harden, and he balls his hands into fists. Tattered and torn and bloody, he's not bowed. I feel heat rising to my chest, which I know I can't one hundred percent attribute to adrenaline, and I feel like I'm staring again, this time at Owen. Funny how your hormones don't care if you're on the threshold of hell.

And while I'm thinking about hormones, Owen and Grant are already running toward the desert. Owen looks back at me. He ticks his head for me to join them, and I see a hint of a smile. His smoke is dark, too. Thick. Settled. I have this bizarre urge to snort it, like some sort of junkie. I think it might give me guts. I rub at my face as if that could straighten out my thoughts. This last half hour has given me enough fodder for a decade of sleepless rendezvous with 3:00 a.m.

I take off after them, and soon we break through the edge of the camp, the three of us running through the desert at a dead sprint, streaking smoke behind us like the tail of a comet, with Chaco crowing high above us.

We follow Grant's lead, and the kid can run. He seems to know the best route, jumping over pits and pointing out rocks to watch. He's not tiring, and neither is Owen. Or if he is, he's hiding it well. So I don't slow either. I try not to think of the kinds of things that scamper and slither around the desert soaking up the last of the sun. I tell myself it's probably mostly fluffy little prairie dogs, but then I see a flash of banded scales. Not a fluffy prairie dog. There's no stopping now. In fact, I pick up the pace and fall in step with Owen. He's sweating profusely. There is no wind in this desert, and we're baked twice: once from what's left of the sun and once from the heat seeping out of the dirt below.

Grant skids to a stop. Above him, Chaco wheels hard right and flares his feathers out behind us in a low loop. He coasts right over my shoulder and settles on Grant's head. Grant ticks forward with the force of his landing but keeps his eyes focused on a bare patch of land in front of us ringed by caution tape. It's almost a perfect square—I'd say two hundred feet or so per side. The dirt looks hammered down here. Like a big square elephant sat on it. Grant won't go past the tape, and when Owen tries to step past him, Grant tugs him back.

"Is this the place?" I ask. "The thin place?"

Grant nods, his eyes sweeping the flat land. "See that rig over there?" He points at the rig I saw from the distance without looking at it. Now that it's near dark and the rig is lit up, I see at least ten people moving about underneath the spotlights.

"This was where that rig was first set up. 'Cept they couldn't set up right cause the bell was here. They broke a bunch of drill bits. Those cost a ton of cash. So they moved the rig over there."

Chaco chirrups, and Grant nods. "Well, yeah. Other things went wrong too. The rig sort of broke down. It all kind of went to chaos."

Chaco caws.

Grant's eyes are unfocused again. "This is a thin place close to chaos, but it's broken. It's leaking."

"Leaking what?" I ask, still catching my breath.

Grant seems to struggle with this. I can see him talking to Chaco in silence.

"Souls," Grant says. "But not like Pap's soul. Pap is good where he's at. This is the other kind of soul. From the other side of the river. The kind that don't care where they're at."

Rivers and souls aside, I can't see anything. I squint and still can't see anything. Just the desert at sunset, and all I can hear are the distant clanks and calls of men at work.

Beside me, I see Owen squinting too, with his hands on his hips.

"I can't see anything," Owen says, echoing my thoughts. "Are you sure, Grant?"

Chaco chirrups again from Grant's shoulder, and this time he flares out his wings. They reach twice again the width of Grant's shoulders. Grant steps back and holds the fist that clutches the bell out in front of him.

"Chaco says to grab your crows," Grant says.

Owen reaches in his pocket, and I grab my totem at the same time. In an instant, we blink into the thin world. The first thing I notice is Grant, standing like a toy soldier in front of us, his body a faint outline of smoke, but the bell that he holds in his hand blazes like the sun. So does Chaco sitting atop his head. In fact, I don't think I could rightly call Chaco a bird any longer. He's a changing thing. A bird one moment, then a lithe, leonine thing prowling across Grant's shoulders the next before returning to bird form again. The two of them stand like pillars of white against what I see beyond them.

I see the thinning that Grant is talking about. It floats in the air like a swimming pool, reflecting light in crazy, distorting ways. And in the middle, it's leaking. Strange lights float on the far side of the pool. They zip and shake and spin spastically, but they're all slowly moving toward the crack, like hundreds of strange fish pulled toward a leak in a billion-gallon aquarium.

"Get ready," Grant says. "If you have to let go of your crow, get away. Don't let them touch you. And don't worry about me. Chaco says they hate the bell because the bell has rules to it and they hate rules."

Chaco's wings flare out larger than a beach umbrella over Grant. I can feel the subtle pinch of the thin place already starting to squeeze me, but I ignore it. I grab Owen's hand. Owen squeezes back. There is a moment of pure desert silence. Then I hear a powerful splintering sound, like a windshield cracking, and I see the thin place break.

The bobbing lights drop out of the fissure one by one, and as they do, they change. They become a misty black smoke that sifts and clumps together into ever-changing shapes of two- and four-legged creatures. Each of them is different but for one thing. Every one of them has a hollow, swirling black pit where their face should be.

These things look and lurch like monsters from the darkest closet of my imagination, but I don't sense malice from them. The color of their smoke, the way it drips from them, I recognize it. Some of the worst cases I dealt with at Chaco Health Clinic had a touch of it—usually the poor men and women who were beyond themselves with addiction, people who didn't know who they were anymore, only that nothing around them made sense and everything was spiraling out of control. Their new normal was chaos. They had a touch of this black. These things *are* that black.

"If you can push them back through the break, chances are they'll go their own way on the other side," Grant says.

"Chances are?" Owen asks. "That's the best we got?"

"Just kick them back where they came from. We gotta hold them here, in this stretch of desert. No further," Grant says, with boyish simplicity.

Owen looks at me with a wide-eyed, terrified smile. "Hold them here. Why the hell not? Like the little Dutch boy."

He lets out a nervous chuckle, and that's when they seem to notice us. A four-legged thing half trips, half leaps toward Owen as he's talking to me. I step forward and grab it where I guess its neck would be. It shifts and turns in my hands, wriggling like a snake. I scream and drop it. The slimy-but-dry feeling of its scales sets me wiping my free hand on my jeans. I let out a string of *ew*s that I'm not proud of, but what can I say? I hate snakes.

My hopping around draws more of them our way, all of them still shifting but settling on a human form. Owen doesn't let them. He's got his hands up and in fists, one with the crow in it, and he goes boxing. He gets one good, clean uppercut to the first thing then kicks the rest over. He looks a bit like a disgruntled postman taking it out on some boxes, but it works. I watch as he drags one soul back under the break and then drop-kicks it upward. He staggers and winces, limping a bit, but the thing is sucked up, back through the crack. It's like a vacuum. The middle of the break drops the souls out, but the edges suck them back up. It's a balance, albeit a broken one.

Owen turns to me and gives me a look that says *if I can do it, so can you*. Which makes me pull my shoulders back, put my own hands up, and get to work. A smaller form floats over to me, and I catch it with my free hand. It shifts under my grip, first into a four-legged thing of some sort, then a flapping bird, then a hissing rodent. I almost drop it then, but I manage to rear back and chuck it into the updraft, where it's sucked away again. Owen's drop-kicking like it's his job, but still more come. For every one we kick out, two slip in. This is a losing fight.

I notice that when the souls hit the ground they change the ground as well. They create divots and mounds where none were before, like their very touch rewrites the world. Even the air they pass through smears and clouds. I try to get Owen's attention to show him what I mean, but my initial butt-kicking adrenaline is wearing off and the painful pinch of the crow is seeping in. It makes my teeth rattle. I have to let go of my totem.

In a blink I'm back in the living world, standing in the middle of an empty patch of desert. I can't see the souls, but I can see how they muddy the world as they slip through the break in the sky above me. Ten feet away I know Owen struggles with something out of my sight because I can see how it blurs everything around him. Behind me, Grant stands stock still like a tiny shaman, his eyes blank and distant, his bell hand out. Above me, Chaco dives with a screaming call and blinks out of sight and into a battle of his own. I shake my hand off like I touched a hot stove and take in several gulps of hot desert air. I grab my totem again.

Chaco slams into some roiling black shape that looks near enough to a person. It whips and boils around him as he drags it back to the break and flings it in the updraft. Owen is tiring, not only from struggling with the souls but also from the bite of his crow totem. His teeth grind; his face is pale and splotchy. He shoves another creature high into the air. It's sucked away from him, but he staggers and sits hard on the ground before blinking away to the real world. When he flits back to the other side, he's a murky outline to me, but I can clearly see two of the souls focus on him, as if suddenly picking up a different scent. His living, breathing scent. They start to make their way toward him, bulky blocks of smoke that fall into form and shape as they lumber forward, and that he cannot see. Above, Chaco screeches, and Grant translates, his voice shrill and cracking.

"Don't let them touch you in the living world! They'll change you forever if they touch you! You gotta hold the totems!"

Owen seems not to have heard; he's still panting and

flexing the hand that held his totem, now on the desert floor next to him. The souls march nearer to him, ten feet away now, but he can't see them. They've turned the air and the earth around them into rifts and rivets and bubbles and streaks, charring some bits and smoothing others but forever changing everything, and I know that they'll do the same to Owen if they touch him. So I grip my crow tightly, lower my head, and come at them sideways.

The lead figure reaches out to Owen, trailing a sooty mess where its arm passes, and it grabs his lapel before I can slam my shoulder into it. I sink into it like squeezing a sponge, only instead of water coming out, I'm inundated with a muddy blast of chaotic pictures and images until it staggers away from me. My shoulder tingles, but I'm otherwise unchanged.

Owen looks at his shirt collar in horror. It's smeared. Not burned, not tattered or torn or broken, but smeared. Like an impressionist painting. Its essence has been changed.

"Good lord!" Owen says then scrambles to grab his totem. He blinks into the thin world next to me just in time to see the second figure a few feet from him, reaching out to him. It pauses as Owen leaves the living world, almost like it's disappointed. Then Owen grabs it by the neck, spins around so he's behind it, and drags it one-handed back to the updraft. He squats and encircles the thing's trunk with both hands then grunts and heaves it up into the break, where it's sucked away. He reaches for me and grabs my hand, and together we carefully step away, back to Grant. As we do, another soul slips out and another. We blink back to the living world, and I steady myself with both hands on the ground.

"What the hell are these things?" Owen asks.

"Chaco says they're souls that went down the chaos side of the river," Grant says, his voice distant.

"I can feel it, when I touch them in the thin world. I get these—"

"Bad thoughts," Grant finishes.

Owen nods, working his fingers like he's trying to get the blood flow back.

I know even without being able to see them that the souls have turned their attention back toward us. Owen shakes his head.

"The pinch of the thin place is getting worse. It's like one long bee sting," Owen says, gasping in the warm air. "I'm gonna be pretty worthless here after too much longer, but maybe I can lead them away from you guys for a bit. Give you a chance to fix that break."

"Owen." I shake my head, but he interrupts me, even as his eyes flick across the deceivingly empty desert around us. They're coming for us, right now. It makes me wince.

"You're more important than I am, Caroline. Always have been. You can do things nobody else can... maybe you can fix that break."

"No," Grant says, interrupting us both. "If you're tired, stay behind me." Chaco swoops down and lands on his head then turns to us and nods.

"Seriously?" I ask.

Chaco nods hard. "Quick!" Grant says, pleading.

Owen and I look at each other, then at Grant, and then scamper to stand right behind him, each of us with one hand on his shoulder. I take a breath and grip my totem, and when I snap into the thin world I have to stifle a scream.

The souls are surrounding us. I count fifteen of them, maybe ten feet from us and pressing in. I grip Grant's shoulder harder than I mean to and try to focus on breathing as Chaco caws loudly.

"Hold still," Grant says. As if I could move a muscle anyway. The four of us stand as still as statues, like we're posing for some ridiculous family portrait. They shamble forward, and I begin to think that maybe Grant just wanted us all to be together when we're smeared out of existence by these things, but when the first soul gets within a couple of feet of us, the bell starts to glow. It's soft at first but enough to give the souls pause. The closest souls press forward again. But the bell glows brighter with each inch they take, and it's as if the light itself is a hardening barrier. The closer the souls get, the more they struggle, until they're stopped cold inches from us, and the bell is blazing like a spotlight from Grant's fist. It's so bright I have to close my eyes. Chaco caws again, and Grant speaks for him.

"The bell is a symbol of order. It's been passed down forever. It creates each Walker, which is a job that keeps order between the worlds. These things are its opposite. Souls that have chosen chaos. They're like opposite ends of a magnet." He looks up at me and smiles. "Stick with me and they can't touch you."

Owen laughs, his eyes dazzling in the light of the bell. I almost sag with relief, but I don't want even another inch of separation between us.

"Take that, you stupid things!" Grant yells. Chaco fluffs his breast up and titters.

"Yeah, you... frickin' stupid things!" Owen says, steering away from a swear word I know he wants to grab. "You ruined my shirt!"

I find myself laughing, too, especially when I see the chaos souls start to fade back, inching away from us, leaving a greasy stain in their wake. Then something grabs their attention. They all turn as one to the right. I follow their line of sight and see that they've turned to the oil rig in the near distance. An engine has revved to life, and another battery of floodlights have kicked on, illuminating a handful of people working on the platform there. I stop laughing. When the souls begin to move toward the oil rig, Owen does too. Grant falls silent. "Oh, no," I whisper.

"We're not easy prey anymore," Owen says. "So they're moving on to what is."

"We gotta stop 'em," Grant whispers, his voice breaking. "Pap worked on a rig like that once. There's someone else's Pap out there. Maybe a bunch of them."

Chaco caws again and lifts off into the air, wheeling above us. "Chaco says to stay behind the bell, do what we can near the break," Grant says quietly.

"It's like spitting into the wind," Owen says. "There's more by the minute. And they're all heading off toward the rig."

"Unless we can plug that hole, we'll just be running in place," I say.

"Chaco says he's working on that," Grant says. I follow Chaco's flight and watch as he dives straight for the break, changing his own form until he's a pencil-thin streak of black feathers. I squeeze Grant's shoulder even harder as he shoots for the break, and in a blink he's gone. For a second I think maybe he's plugged the hole himself, but half a minute later another black soul slips through and hits the battered and scarred ground below the break. Another follows. They form themselves, take one look at us, and then head off in the direction of the rig with the others.

"I think it may be up to us," Owen says.

15

THE WALKER

I thought about jumping. I don't want you thinking that I just counted that out, because that makes me sound like a chicken. But you tell me what you would do in my situation. First of all, the agents are long gone. They were long gone the minute they ducked under the river. The second thing is that I'm in pain for the first time in a while. My jaw feels like a balloon where Douglas hit me, and my knee is all swollen where the earth slammed into it on its way to taking me up into the sky and plunking me here on this magic-carpet-sized mesa about a hundred feet up.

I know I can't die. I'm already dead. When I lose this job, I'll become just another soul in the river—and I pray to who or whatever runs this place that I float the other way when that time comes—but even knowing this, I'm still not so sure that jumping off a hundred-foot cliff would be good for me. And don't get me started on how I'd be jumping in water. You ever jump off a big cliff? The Chaco flats flooded one time when Joey and I were thirteen, and this deep desert pool formed in the middle of the valley for a while. All the kids liked to jump into it from the cliff edges. On a dare, I jumped from what I swore at the time was fifty feet, but now I'm thinking it was more like twenty. I didn't pencil my legs right, and when I hit, I tweaked my knee and got a slap right to the balls that I felt for the next three months. At this height, water turns to cement. Maybe not soul-river water, but still…

The third thing is, the whole landscape is bucking and shifting at random, and I have this terrible feeling that as soon as I chuck myself off this cliff it'll shift and melt, and I'll become a smashed bug for no reason.

So that's why I'm still up here. If you're wondering. Now that I hear myself, it does sort of sound chickenshit. I wonder what Caroline would think of me, flat as a door on this mesa, batting back and forth the idea of jumping. She'd see right through me. That's her gift. She'd see that I'm really thinking about whether it matters in the long run anyway. I'm either solo up here forever or solo down there forever. Say I catch the agents, stop them from ruining things, then what? It's back to the solo workday. Forever. Neither choice gets me closer to her.

Plus, what Parsons said back when the bell rang still stings a bit. Here I was thinking that the agents wanted my job so bad that they'd go to the ends of the earth and beyond for it, but it turns out they just wanted to get beyond the veil. Then he called me a day-laboring peasant.

What an asshole.

All I'm saying is things have me in kind of a funk right now. I know that time is precious, but I'm getting jaded. Time is slowly losing its importance to me. I'm like the annoying guru at the top of the mountain who pisses off the pilgrims. Everyone dies at one time or another. Sure, they may bottleneck at the veil without me there to snip their lines, but why not just sit on a fucking rock until the dam bursts?

Anyway, I'm not proud of it, but that's what I'm thinking on my rock, when out of the corner of my eye I spy a long slice of black shoot from the river, like the edge of an obsidian knife. As I watch, the back half of the slice catches up with the front half to form a beak and tail feathers, and two wings shoot out with an audible bang. I hop up. It's Chaco! I suspected Chaco might be able to travel through the break, but I didn't dare hope he'd come for me. I leap up and wave my hands.

"Hey! Over here! Chaco!" I laugh and then cut it short as a wave of vertigo hits me, or maybe the plateau shifts a little. I have to catch my balance. Then I get to waving again. "Over here!"

Chaco wheels around. "Yeah, yeah. I see you. I see you," he says. And he doesn't sound happy. I step back, and he lands in a fit of dust at my feet, flaps his wings a few times before tucking them in, then just stares up at me.

"What?" I ask.

"Where are the agents? I only ask because I swear when I last saw you, you were going after them. And yet here you are without them."

"They jumped in the river." Chaco follows where I point and furrows the fine feathers on his head. He turns back to me.

"And what the fuck are you doing? Working on your tan?"

"No," I say, fully aware I sound like a child. "It's just... I dunno... did you know I can get hurt here? What's up with that?"

"Of course you can get hurt here. This is the doorway to chaos. The rules don't apply. Or if they do, it's on and off.

Nothing is for sure. I'd have thought the freaky landscape might have tipped you off on that one."

"Well, that's another thing, I thought maybe this plateau would... sort of... go back down." I'm reaching now.

"Or stay up here for eternity," Chaco says. "Which it has an equal chance of doing. Given that there are no rules here."

I know I don't have much of a leg to stand on, so I do what I always do when pressed against the wall. I get pissed. It helps, a little. "Hey, fuck you, man. Excuse me if I have to think about it for a bit before I throw myself off a cliff. You're not on this side of the coin."

I should know by now that this type of shit doesn't work on Chaco.

"Do you have any idea what is going on in the mortal world right now?" he asks, clawing his way up my front until he's right in my face. I open my mouth then close it. I assume things are going downhill fast, but I don't really know. I don't really know anything about what is going on, to be honest.

"Owen and Caroline are standing with Grant against a frickin' platoon of chaos souls. A platoon, Walker. They're coming from a break in the thin place where the bell landed. It's sourced directly from this end of the river. Right down there. And if we don't close it, I got reason to believe all the thin places will start to break down. Everywhere."

"What are chaos souls?" I ask quietly, my mind racing.

Chaco turns to the river and points with his wing. "Those are chaos souls. This side of the river is chock full of them. The river only exists on this plane, but it's very deep. Sometimes it gets close to other planes. There are thin places where the bottom of that river gets too close to the living world, and the thin places are cracking because those two assholes have been screwing with things. The river is leaking, and your friends are caught up in it." He's puffing rapidly now.

"Chaos souls..." I repeat. That doesn't sound good. "Are those like... like demons or something?" The Navajo believe that demons are trapped souls that wander the earth. It fits. But Chaco shakes his head.

"Demons," he says, as if I'm stuck in the Stone Age. "What did you see when you first came through with Abernathy?"

"Nothing. I mean, a shore. The river. It was calm."

"No judge, no jury weighing Ab's life?"

"No."

"No winged St. Peter behind his ledger, looking your name up, running your life down, telling you which way to go?"

"No. Ab seemed to know which way to go. He felt called to the other side."

Chaco nods. "Toward the side of order. The side of light. That's because that's the kind of man he was in life. But if you happened to cross over with any of those guys down there, they'd tell you that it just felt right for them to go toward the other side. This side. Where you are right now. Sitting on your ass."

I look down on the churning souls below. "So they're here of their own accord."

"That's right. These souls brought themselves here. They aren't demons, they aren't ghosts, they're souls that feel that the end of this side of the river is where they belong. Now if that's damned, so be it. Damned can mean a lot of things in my book."

"What's at the end of this side of the river?"

Chaco settles his feathers for the first time. Sort of

slumps a bit. "That's something you gotta find out for your-self. Because that's where the agents went."

I know Chaco knows what's at the end of the river. "Is it... is it a lonely place?" I ask. I know full well how lame it sounds coming out. I also know I'm showing my hand to Chaco. Showing him what's really bothering me. So it's good of him when he softens his bird brow. He understands.

"It's a place of chaos, Walker. Sometimes lonely, some-times not. What I do know is that it's never one thing for long. It's not a place of peace."

"And I gotta go there, huh?"

"If you don't, the living world you knew will be overrun. The girl you love will be wiped away forever. These souls don't just want chaos. When they're this far down the river, they *are* chaos. They rewrite everything they touch in the living world. You and I both know Caroline. We know she's a soul that would follow Ab's path down the river. But if one of those things touches her, they could change her, and she'd be powerless to stop it. Maybe she'd end up down there. Maybe she'd be of two minds, ripped apart."

I find myself locking my jaw. I find myself balling my fists. I step to the edge. And damn if it isn't still just as far down.

"I know what you're thinking, Walker. You've been running through a *woe is me* scenario up here. You're getting the itch. I've seen it before, with past Walkers. It's really hitting you now that you are all you've got out here. You're getting thoughts that aren't like you. Thoughts like 'What is it to me if the world goes to hell?' But you gotta remember, man. Remember them. Remember her. And she's not alone. But if things go wrong here—and they're going very wrong right now, my man—if they keep it up, she could be lost forever. Do you want that? Remember her."

And I do. I remember her. It's the color of her soul string that I remember first. The *colors*, actually, because she has way more than one. I got to see them for a bit, before I left. The best way I can describe them is like the swirling colors on the skin of a floating bubble when the sunlight catches it just right. And then I think of that bubble popping. Or worse, being *smeared* somehow. Smudged out by the chaos souls dripping from the crack at the bottom of the river. The river I gotta jump into.

"Fine. Fuck it. For her," I say. "See you, Chaco."

And I jump.

I fall a long time. It's like the land drops out below me, farther and farther. I tell myself not to flail, but I flail. I flail like a ragdoll. I scream too. Guess I haven't learned anything since the Chaco flats jump. I get ready for another ball whacking.

But then, just when I can see the souls roiling the water, I feel Chaco's claws on my back, ripping my shirt to get a grip under my arms, and the earth stops rushing at me. Instead it only zooms. Then it floats toward me.

"Chaco! You could do this the whole time?"

"Yep," Chaco says, his big beak above my head. "But I had to see if you would jump."

Before I can piece together the weight behind that statement, Chaco says, "Good luck, Walker. Give 'em hell." And he drops me into the river.

16

GRANT ROMER

Back before Mom and Dad died, the three of us and Pap would sometimes go to church. Mostly for Easter and Christmas, but sometimes Mom would get the idea to go on a random Sunday, so I've been to church a bunch of times. After Mom and Dad died, I think Pap kinda turned on the whole thing, so the two of us never went. But I still remember Sunday school, and I know about souls and how they're the real *you* inside you. Chaco says these black smoke monsters are souls, but if they are, they sure ain't any kind of soul I've ever heard of.

I always thought that you got your soul, and if you believe in God and do all right with your life, you'll end up in Heaven and get to see your mom and dad and pap again. If you don't do those things, well, you'll be sorry and sent to Hell. These chaos souls sure look like they come from Hell. But they don't look sorry. They don't look like they're burning or hollerin' in pain, neither. I'll tell you what they look like: they look like sick animals. Crazy, smoking animals that are wandering around doing what they do because that's all they know now. Like the mangy, rabid coyotes that sometimes come in from the desert and have to be put down.

When that bunch of them got real close to Caroline, Owen, Chaco, and me, I didn't feel like they wanted to get at *me,* Grant Romer. They wanted to get at everything that made it so I was standing there in that spot. It was like the bell formed a little snow globe around us, and the chaos souls wanted to turn all of us to water and mix up the snow globe so there wasn't nothin' recognizable in it but a bunch of bits. They weren't angry about it, or scary like the agents are scary. I think it's just what they are.

And what they're doing right now is heading straight for a drilling rig, like ants to a kitchen. I think it's the noise—or maybe the smell—but mostly the way it's all working together: people and machine. There's no chaos there. But it's coming. The souls are messin' up the desert where they step and screwing up the sky where they pass. One steps through a tumbleweed, and the tumbleweed stretches out like putty until it's a dripping line.

"We can't just sit here and watch all those men get smeared," I say. "I don't care what Chaco said."

I look up at Caroline and Owen, and they both nod.

"Really?" I ask. "You ain't gonna try to stop me or nothin'?"

"He said stay behind the bell. He didn't say where the bell could go," Caroline says. "I know we can't stop these things; there's too many of them. But what we can do is warn those men at least."

"Convince a bunch of good ol' boy roughnecks that an army of cell-destroying chaos souls is at their doorstep," Owen says. "Sounds easy enough." He's rolling up his sleeves. I can't tell if he's joking or if he's dead serious. I'm beginning to think with him it's always a little bit of both, because Caroline smiles.

"Leave the convincing to me," Caroline says. "I'll know what to say."

Owen looks at her then looks down at me. I shrug. I've seen weirder things today.

"Let's roll," Owen says. "You're in the lead, big guy. We follow you."

I start running toward the rig and thinking about giraffes again, and then all of a sudden I'm crying. Thankfully we're running pretty fast, and I'm in the lead so Caroline and Owen don't see.

The last of the sun still shines off the tip of the rig. The giraffe stands tall, but if the chaos souls get to it, it won't for much longer. For everything to be okay, so many different parts have to keep working together. Especially the blowout preventer, the guts of the giraffe that kept Pap safe. It has to keep working to keep these men safe too.

We cut wide around the march of the souls. Caroline holds on to my hand, and every now and then Owen stops, grabs his crow, and checks to make sure we won't run into any of the souls and wipe ourselves out by mistake. We keep running, and he catches up a little bit sweatier each time with some added directions. *Cut left. Shoot straight through. This is the front of them. Now they're behind us.*

The sun is nearly set now, and the shadows are long. I look behind us and see a flat stretch of desert that's shifting and moving in little ways with the touch of the souls, like it's made of new paint that's getting rained on. You might miss it if you didn't know what to look for, but once you see it, it's impossible to unsee. It's like the desert is playing tricks on us.

"How far back are they?" Caroline asks. The hands we hold are sweaty, but she hasn't let go, and neither have I.

"Closest one is about fifty yards or so. They're wandering but with a purpose. I think we've got five or so minutes max to get all these people out of here," Owen says. Then he looks at Caroline. "What do you need from me?"

Caroline scans the rig. It's loud and smells like gas. She squints, looking for something beyond what we can see, but she shakes her head. "We gotta get someone who's in charge."

"Oh, I can do that!" I say. "He'll be in the toolbox. C'mon." I grab their hands and pull them after me toward the side where there's a shed. A few men in hard hats look at us with questions in their eyes, but we ignore them and they don't say anything. I stop in front of a makeshift staircase made out of big bricks that leads to an open door. I hop up and in the shed with Caroline and Owen close behind. Inside, three men stare at a bunch of computers with all sorts of numbers and shapes running up the screen. All three wear hard hats, but two of them are in nice clothes, and one is in a greasy brown monkey suit. He has a big brown beard with bits of grey in it, and his hands are tanned and thick and strong like Pap's. I run up to him.

"Excuse me, sir. Are you the tool pusher?" I ask. He looks to his right above my head, then he looks down.

"What the fu... heck is this? Sam, is this your kid?" he asks.

One of the two men sitting down swivels around. He blinks at me. "No. This yours, Don?" The other man turns around for a second then turns back.

"I don't have kids," he says.

"He's with us," Caroline says.

"And who are you?" the tool pusher asks. "This is a tight

hole, ma'am. That means no visitors allowed. And it certainly ain't no place for a kid."

"You're in danger," Caroline says, stepping forward, stopping him. "You and your whole crew. All of you need to leave this place now. It's life or death."

This gets everyone's attention. Both men swivel back around. The tool pusher squints at us. He has the same lines shooting from the sides of his eyes that Pap had, and I almost step closer to him. But then I feel Owen squeeze my shoulder a bit, and I fight the feeling down. Pap would be the first to say that this ain't the time for stuff like that.

"Who the hell put you up to this?" one of the clean men asks. "Did corporate do this? This shit isn't funny."

"No, it's not," Owen says. "You have less than five minutes to get everyone off this rig." His voice is rising, but Caroline stops him with a touch. She hasn't stopped looking at the tool pusher. I mean *looking* at him. The way she looked at me that helped me get up off Pap when Pap was gone.

"You know what I'm talking about, don't you?" Caroline says.

The tool pusher shakes his head, but I can tell she's getting to him. If anything, he looks scared. Caroline steps forward, and he steps back.

"Now just a minute," the other clean man says, getting up from his seat, but Owen steps in front of him.

"Sit down, kid," he says. Which is funny, because he doesn't look like a kid to me. He looks about the same age as Owen. But the guy listens. He sits down.

"Nothing about this operation has been going right," Caroline says, looking carefully at the tool pusher. "You had to move the rig, even. Things are breaking. Your veteran men are screwing up." The tool pusher licks his lips and straightens his hat, his eyes on her. "You think you've lost it. You're wondering if you're too old. You think maybe the men don't respect you anymore. That you can't do your job."

The tool pusher lets out this tiny little huff of breath, like he was hugged real hard.

"It's not your equipment, it's not your men, and it sure as heck isn't you. It's this place. And this place just broke open. Now, please. For the love of God. Get your men and yourselves out of here." Caroline stands up straight again. It's quiet for a couple of seconds.

"Sound the alarm, Don," the tool pusher says quietly.

"What? Just because some crazy lady came in here and—"

"Sound the goddamn alarm! Clear the floor! Get everyone out! Now!"

"Just calm down, Jerry—"

"Oh, for fuck's sake," Jerry says, pushing the man aside as he flips open a box and presses a big red button. An alarm goes off that sounds like a truck horn on repeat. He looks back at us, eyes wide. "You better be right, ma'am, or you just cost us a boatload of money. And our jobs."

But Caroline isn't looking at him, and I'm not sure she even hears him. Her head is cocked like she's straining to hear something out the door. I run to the doorway, but I can't see anything but bright lights and, beyond that, complete blackness. Desert night and worse. But I don't need to see anything to hear the screaming.

All six of us rush out of the toolbox and look around to see where it's coming from, which is probably why none of the workers notice when Caroline and Owen disappear into the thin place to get a better look. They're back in a blink.

"Over there," Owen says. He's pointing at the butt of the giraffe, and it's blowing a lot of smoke. Way too much smoke. The screaming is coming from the men on the drilling floor. I know it's the smoke that's scaring them, but if they looked carefully they'd have a lot more to scream about. The engine is smoking because it's being warped. And it's being warped because a chaos soul is walking right through it, trying to get to the men on the platform. With each step, the metal and gears and belts change, some to sand, some to drippy goop, some to black smoke. It looks like a big thumb is slowly wiping right through it.

The tool pusher and his friends take off toward it before any of us can scream at them to stop, but they get about ten feet before the engine catches fire. It's just a little fire, just a lick of a thing, but a fire on a rig is very, very bad.

"Clear the rig!" the tool pusher screams, waving his hands. He cuts right and grabs a red spray-bottle fire extinguisher while the other two just sort of stand there staring at it. He blows right past them with the big bottle in his hand, fiddling with a lever on top.

"He's gonna run right into them," Owen says. He turns to Caroline. "Stay here with Grant. I'll be back." Before Caroline or I can say anything, he puts his hand in his pocket and disappears. I try to step forward, but Caroline holds me tight. I look up at her, and I can see in her eyes that she's holding herself as still as she is me. She wants to be out there with him.

"I'm just gonna look," she says. "I'll still be right here." She disappears too. I watch the tool pusher running around hell-bent on getting to that fire. He has the spray bottle out in front of him. Caroline comes back. Her face is white. "They're all over," she says.

"Owen?" I ask.

"He's fighting them, but he can only push them away. He's gonna get overwhelmed."

Owen just about scares the snot out of the tool pusher when he blinks back right in front of him and takes him out at the waist. Both of them go down to the ground in a mess of limbs. Owen presses him flat, like a big invisible axe is passing over them both, and I bet in a lot of ways it probably is.

"Forget the fire!" I hear Owen scream. "It's too late for that! Go!"

The tool pusher is sitting as if he just fell smack off his bike and onto the concrete, and he's checking to see if he's still in one piece. So Owen just gets behind him and pulls him up and out of the way, his boots dragging through the dirt. And good thing too, 'cause that's when the engine starts making this heavy hammering sound, then a whine, and then it blows to pieces.

There are still men on the giraffe's back when the engine blows. It smacks all of them flat as pancakes. At first I think they're all dead because the bell gets heavy and I can feel it come together. I hold it real still until it passes. Then two of the men start to move on the ground, and I see the smearing of chaos souls moving toward them. The souls didn't stop at the engine. They don't want the engine. They want the people. At least three souls are cutting their way toward the crew like nails slowly scraping through butter. The giraffe makes a big groan, and its neck bobs a little to the right. I look back at the men crawling around on the platform. Sure, they could be like the guys at the man camp that said mean things to Owen and Caroline. But maybe they're guys like Pap. Little Paps. Working at becoming tool pushers. Guys with grandsons.

"I can't let them die," I say. And I run. I slip through Caroline's grip like we're playing Red Rover. She screams after me, but I'm pretty fast, and I'm already halfway across the grounds in a flash. I feel a whump of air to my right, and then she's right there keeping pace.

"I'm the only one that can keep the souls away from them," I say, before she can get mad at me. I glance up at her. She's not mad at me. She wants this as much as I do. We go wide around the body of the giraffe and up the metal steps on the far side from the engine fire. I'm up top first. There are three men, two of them rolling around and crying and one not moving at all. The souls are slicing butter our way. They're just a couple of feet from the one that's not moving. I start to go to him when Caroline grabs me.

"No," she says, and her voice is heavy. "He's gone. These other two. Stand in front of them."

So I do. I stand in front of them with my feet apart and set and my hands on my hips, and I feel the bell start to shine in my fist. Behind me, Caroline corrals the two men until they're in a row at my back, then she comes back to me and puts her arm around me. She squeezes. It makes me puff out my chest more.

The two men are shaking it off, touching their bodies and poking at their ears because I bet they can't hear nothin' but ringing. One gets up and weaves away behind us and off the platform, but the other has a cut-up leg. He left a trail of blood when Caroline dragged him behind me. He tries to scoot away, but Caroline grabs him by the scruff and leans down and whispers something. His eyes get all big, but he stays put. The three of us watch as the souls reach the dead man. One cuts right through him. It's exactly like you'd expect and worse. Just this past Fourth of July I brought out my firework collection and my bucket of army men and played war with 'em. I dug a pit in the sand out back of Pap's house and started a fireworks fire with a bunch of sparklers and threw in a few of the army men to watch them melt. I picked one up with a sparkler and it stuck to it, so I wiped it off on the wood edge of the sandbox. This is just like that, only more red. The man behind us screams, but he stays put. Thank God the guy was dead. If he wasn't, I'd probably be screaming right with him.

The bell shines real bright, enough to make me squint, and I know that the chaos souls are here. Right next to me. Maybe inches from me.

"Stay still!" Caroline yells. All three of us do. It's just like back in the desert. They can't get to me or any of us. But back there it was solid earth we were standing on. Here, it's a sheet of metal above the ground. It starts to bubble where I know the soul is standing. Then it melts and flakes away, turning to ash and dripping to sand at the same time. One hole forms then another, and the souls drop below the platform like a hot iron through ice, leaving a muddy, dead-bug streak behind them. Which would be good, 'cept that they're dropping on the guts of the giraffe.

I look down through the holes and see the drill pipe slice in two, and all of a sudden the giraffe is barfing oil. It blows out high in the air in one big black spew, and then it shuts off just as quick. The blowout preventer clamped it down, and I have enough time to wipe my face and eyes off and look back down to see the blowout preventer start to bubble and shift like a soul is sitting right on top of it.

I look up at Caroline. She sees it too. The man behind us is throwing a fit. It sounds like he's making enough racket for two men. I turn my head to tell him to shush, but I see he's looking up the neck of the giraffe. I follow his eyes, and sure enough, there's another man. Way up high in the crow's nest. Sitting right on the head of the giraffe. He was probably repairing a line or something up there, which is just terrible luck. I don't know why he hasn't used the escape route. They usually have a zip line that leads all the way to the ground, but then I see the line dangling off the side like a leash, useless. At first I think he's hollerin' to get us to save him, but then I see he's hollerin' and pointing at the engine, because it's leaking gas in a long, burning line that's running right toward the bubbling guts of the giraffe.

17

THE WALKER

The first thing I realize when I hit the water, other than that I want to hug my bird friend and punch him in the beak at the same time, is the feel of the souls.

The "water" isn't even water, so to speak. It's not wet. Which makes sense. I assumed this setup was a bit more complex than a bunch of souls floating down a river like rubber ducks. The feeling isn't so different from the soul map, actually, the sense of being totally enveloped by a place. But with the soul map I'm sewing up the strings of those that leave—tucking away their connection to the living world. It's cosmic housekeeping. The soul itself I don't deal with anymore, because I send it here.

Well, here they all are. And, man oh man, do I have to deal with them. I try for a pencil- straight landing but screw it up and hit the river at a jackknife. And I'm surrounded by souls. Not all of them can get out of my way. Not all of them want to get out of my way. And the ones I end up touching sizzle with images and echoes of the lives and experiences that made them what they are.

I don't think it'll surprise you when I say they are in complete chaos.

Each brush against a soul brings me a rapid-fire slideshow of pictures that makes no sense to me. A car wreck as seen by a pedestrian, a slab of snow breaking from the side of a mountain, a roiling anthill, a broken tile set among a thousand whole tiles, a stream of water blown by the wind. Things like that, but millions of them, all in a blink. And there's a feeling, too, coming from each of them. It's just an imprint, an echo, but it's there. Each is a shade different, but they all rub me the same way. The closest I can come to explaining it is this: You know that feeling you get when you're driving your car and you come up on a wreck and you know it's a bad one? That feeling that you don't want to see what happened, but you do at the same time? Everybody has a little bit of that tendency in them. Back on patrol in Chaco, we'd get bad wrecks on the straightaways north through the flats, and sometimes we'd have to have one officer whose sole job it was to keep the rubberneckers moving through. It's human nature to have some interest in the mess and the destruction. Well, these souls have a lot more than just *some* interest. The feeling I get is that these are the guys that would stop traffic whole. Or maybe even cause another wreck from looking too hard. They feed off of it.

And after a while, it gets to me. I feel my own brain turning a bit. I'm getting panicky. I take a bunch of deep breaths, but I keep running into souls. They're everywhere, all around me, lighting the river a fogged-over, electric white. It takes me a bit to position myself to best avoid them. I shift and arch, ducking low and swimming high. The souls only illuminate more souls as I drop further. The pressure doesn't change, but the souls do thin out a bit as I go lower. I touch for the bottom with my toes. It feels spongy and soft, but it holds me. I start walking.

I get to the break Chaco was talking about after just a few minutes. The souls are slowly spinning around it, sort of like when you swirl water around a bottle and create a tornado. This is much more subtle, but it's here. The break is pulling the souls down into it. I watch one spin slowly, like a floating leaf, down, down, and then disappear. I walk up to the spot with caution. After all it took to get me here in the first place, the last thing I want to do is get sucked out.

I stand just outside of the pull and crouch down. The break is really more like a jagged tear. I wish there was something I could do to plug it somehow, but there's nothing here. The closer I get, the more pieces break away. I can see through it to the darkness beyond, and it's different from the darkness of the bottom of the river. It's a dark I know. A desert dark. I get the feeling that in order to close this thing, I'm gonna have to get rid of the agents and the knife first.

I stand. Above me, another soul is caught in a slow, looping spiral downward. I skirt the edge of the break and pick up the pace down the riverbed. The souls zip and shiver and buzz and weave all around me. I keep my hands up in front of my face, partly out of self-defense and partly because I don't want to run into anything. From my perch on high, I saw that the river flattened to nothing not too far from where I jumped in—for whatever that's worth in a world that changes from moment to moment.

And just like that, I'm at the end. I don't hit a wall or a dam but a cavern. A huge, domed cavern. The river feeds into it at the bottom of one side. I thought the river was big, but now it looks like a little stream trickling into the ocean. I can see through the ether of the place, up, up, and all around myself. I feel like I'm a grain of sand inside a giant eggcup, the kind Gam used to have a pair of—porcelain things she always kept clean but that I never saw her use. Countless souls light the cavern a pulsing, electric blue. And hanging from the center of this massive eggcup is a big, black pearl that would fit nicely inside of a crater. It hangs like an earring and shines with a wicked black patina, and it's where all the souls are going. It's also where I see Parsons and Douglas.

The agents stand out like two floating specks of black in a snow globe on crack. Also, the souls seem to want no part of them, and especially no part of what I see in Parsons's hand, glowing green like a toxic splinter.

"Hey!" I yell. My voice is scratchy, and I clear my throat. "Hey, assholes! What do you think you're doing with that thing?" I kick off the ground and push myself forward, swimming up in the cavern, but they're even farther away than I thought. It takes a second for my voice to reach them, but it does, and Parsons turns around briefly. He has the book in one hand and the knife in the other, and at that moment, he slams the book closed and passes it to Douglas, says a few words, then takes off himself, pushing upward, skirting the shimmering black surface of the massive pearl on his way to the top.

"Parsons! Whatever you're doing, cut that shit out right now! Don't be a dumbass! This place is way too powerful for you, or me, or any of us. None of us should be here!"

Parsons isn't stopping. He's floating up, his suit billowing around him. I can see the bone white of his legs above his black socks. I kick harder. I'm coming up on Douglas now. Fucking Douglas. Always my roadblock. How many times am I gonna have to run into this guy? He pops his shoulders back and squares up at me, but all I can look at is this big pearl. It's hypnotizing, so big that the curvature seems flat, and it shines like a black mirror. I feel like I get a taste of what drives moths to a flame. It takes an effort to pull up, to go after Parsons. Which is what Douglas was waiting for, of course, because he plows into me right as I stretch upward.

I fold over him like a piece of paper, and the two of us go spinning back out into the soup of souls. I lose my breath for a second, but without anything hard to land on, we just spin out into nothing until we slow down. He swings at me, but the momentum of pulling the punch back pushes him backward too. When he throws it, I block, and he does a somersault over my right shoulder.

Forget him. It's Parsons who has the knife. Parsons who's fixing to do something stupid. I kick off back toward the pearl, leaving Douglas behind.

"Parsons! Do you *want* to destroy the world? Is that what gets you off?" I kick harder, and I'm getting close until Douglas grabs my ankle. He yanks me backward and sails over my shoulder to try and get between me and Parsons, but I'm not about to let that happen. I grab his balls as his crotch floats over me and yank him backward again. I crush 'em up a bit for good measure. He curls around himself and groans, spinning in a crouch out to my right. Parsons is two-thirds of the way up the pearl. I go into sprint mode.

I'm sweating like a pig, swimming my ass off through nothing, surrounded by souls. While I gasp for whatever passes as air in this place, I notice what the souls are doing. They're thinking. At least, that's what it looks like they're doing. They're spinning around the pearl thinking, and when they've thought hard enough, they either back off, flowing back toward the river, or they shoot forward and hit the pearl, cracking like eggs. I see it happen right in front of me. A soul zooms by and smacks into the pearl, spreading out like a yoke until it's absorbed and becomes part of the thing.

"Parsons! Hey! You pansy ass! Come fight me!" I scream, gasping and swimming. Hurling insults: the last refuge of the truly desperate. It's not the first time I've been here, but it's definitely the worst. Parsons doesn't buy it. I know he can hear me, but he doesn't care about me. I chance a look over my shoulder. Sure enough, there's Douglas. It's like he's on PCP. Nothing stops the guy. At least he has stubby little legs. He's not gaining on me.

But I'm gonna be too late. I know it. I think I knew it before I even entered this place. I think about what Abernathy said. How he asked if I'd ever considered whether maybe a knife that destroys the plan might also be part of the plan. True or not, right now it doesn't make me feel any better.

I scramble up the pearl, my hands and feet slipping. To either side of me, souls slam into its glossy surface. I get a little soul splashback. It's like climbing a mirror. I churn my hands and feet, anything to get speed. Then I get too much speed. I fly past Parsons at the top and let out a string of curse words. I flare out like a skydiver above the pearl, trying to slow myself. And that's how I see Parsons win—me floating above him like some sort of sweaty flying squirrel while he stands at the top of the pearl, holding on with one hand to the thin strand that connects the pearl to the top of the cavern. He watches me sail past without interest. Without joy. Without hate. He watches me like I'm a fly buzzing the picnic, on my way to do fly things.

There's a sleeve in the strand anchoring the pearl. Sort of like a pachinko machine, where you'd drop a token and watch it bounce off the pegs, only this thing has one path and one path only, and it runs down the outer side of the pearl. It's the only seam that I can see on the pearl, which is otherwise an alien sort of perfect. Parsons takes the knife and slaps it broadside against the sleeve. He looks up at me again with his dead eyes.

"Parsons. Please. Whatever this thing is, let it lie." My voice is weak. I wouldn't convince myself. And I realize it's because I'm scared shitless again. "There's nothing but destruction in there," I say. And I know it's true.

For the first time, I think Parsons really sees me. He doesn't gloat or smile or laugh triumphantly. None of that. He actually shakes his head.

"No destruction," he says. "Only chaos." As if the two were different. As if I should understand that.

Then he drops the knife.

It slides with purpose, like it was built for that slot. An absurdly out-of-place memory hits me of when I used to play with a marble track as a kid. You dropped marbles onto it, and they'd slide up and down and around a roller coaster track depending on where you dropped them. They stuck like glue to that track. This is like that. The knife slides as smoothly as water down a spout until it hits a chunk of something, then it starts to hiss and bubble. I kick my way down after it until I get close and can see the stoppage is a chunk of rock on top of rock on top of rock like rolled steel, a lock as thick as my thigh. The kind of thing that would stand the test of eternity, unless you had the pick. And the knife is the pick. It burns into it, sizzling brightly like an acetylene torch under water. And it's working.

Before I can reach the knife, it cuts through the rock, breaking it in two. The pearl splits open a tiny bit. I see the fissure, and then I feel the fissure like the kickback of Dad's old twelve-gauge shotgun we used to shoot at yucca in the desert. I reach for the knife, but it slides out of reach, on its way down to the next lock. This one is bigger, nearly the size of my entire body. I think I can catch it there.

Unless Douglas grabs me around the neck, of course. I spin my leg around in a big, looping roundhouse kick that's meant for his face, but he catches that, too. "Dammit, Douglas! If this is how the world ends, if it's because of guys like you, I'm gonna be really pissed off."

Douglas is smiling at me. It's a vacant, black smile shot through with brittle, white teeth. Whatever these two men once were, they aren't that anymore. They've hit ground zero. DEFCON 1. I pull the leg Douglas holds into my body and then snap out with my free foot. It's a pull-push combo, and it hits home hard. Douglas explodes off of me, spread-eagled and floating, falling, spinning until he's far out in the souls and beyond my sight.

I turn back to the knife. It's already halfway through the second lock. My own kick pushed me back a ways, so it takes me a second to get back to where I was and then far too long to get close to the knife. It's almost as if the knife is getting sharper as it cuts, like it's hitting its stride. It even looks different. It's no longer the homemade hack job I saw back in the desert. It's gone military. It reminds me unsettlingly of the scalp knife Danny Ninepoint always carried around with him. The knife that killed my grandmother and my father. And then it cuts through the second lock.

This time it's no shotgun blast that we get. It's a straight-up underwater explosion. It throws me end over end away from the pearl and out into the ether. I don't know which way is up. All I can do is spread out and hope the spinning stops, and when my body finally does stop, it takes another good while for my head to stop spinning. When I right myself, I'm at least a football field away from the pearl.

Like I said. I failed. Whatever it was I was hoping to do

here, I didn't do it. Now the only thing left is to see how badly I failed.

The only comfort I have is that it looks like Parsons and Douglas were no more prepared for that explosion than I was. Douglas is about a hundred feet below me, shaking his head and treading ether like he's about to go under. I think Parsons had some sort of grand idea of standing on top of the pearl while his master plan came to be, but that ain't happenin' anymore. He got thrown damn near a hundred feet past me, and he's still spinning. He has that floppy-ragdoll look of someone who's been knocked out.

I want to scream at them, but I don't think there's any *them* anymore. I think they've become tools, and there's no use screaming at your screwdriver. You just look like a fool. Instead I look back at the pearl. There is one more lock. This one is as big as a car. I can see the tiny white light of the knife burning through it, and it's already halfway done.

I don't know what kind of opinion you've formed of me by now. I'm sure it's not *great*, but I hope it's not garbage either. So I hope you'll understand me when I say I'm not the type of guy to go running into oblivion and believe me when I tell you that going after that knife would be oblivion right now. A stupid, foolish, admirable gesture of suicide.

That's not me.

I'm more the type of guy who says if the world is gonna end when that pearl opens, we need to find a way to tackle that problem on level footing. Not floating and spinning. In other words, I have this stupid notion that there's gonna be another day. Maybe that's what comes with a job that gives you a zillion and one days. And that's why I start booking it back toward the river entrance where I came in. My back is to the pearl when the final lock blows. I'd say it goes with about the strength of a car wreck, but I've never been in a car wreck. That's just the biggest, wrenching trauma I can think of in the silent, blue moment before the concussion wave hits me. It's like I'm a puppet getting yanked off stage, but instead of going up, I go down and out. Ass first and half-conscious, I'm flushed out of the eggcup and back into the river, along with a million souls, both agents, and—I catch a glimpse of it—the knife as well, glowing brighter than anything around me. I land on hard ground and flop around like a prize catch in some hick dynamite-fishing contest.

I black out. I'm not sure for how long but not long enough for the aching and buzzing to subside. Caroline's voice echoes in my ears, and it sounds close, but my mind has played tricks on me before where Caroline is concerned. The ground under me shudders and keeps shuddering, which is what I think finally brings me back. I roll over on my stomach. Everything hurts in that way your body hurts before a really disgusting set of bruises shows up. The kind of bruises you have a really hard time explaining away. I'm gonna get those bruises, and I'm dead. That's how bad it is.

I expect to see the river, but what I do see is a trickle of a stream. The rest of the river is gone, and I'm lying on the dry riverbed. Splayed out not even twenty feet from me are the agents. They aren't moving. Around them a few souls linger like beached jellyfish.

In the middle of them all is the knife.

My first thought is to get to the knife, and I do try, but my body won't quite respond. I honestly think if I was alive, I'd be dead for sure after that, but since I'm already dead, my body has to adjust to being dead twice, which it isn't too happy about. I manage a few flops in the knife's direction before I have to steady my head again.

My second thought is to wonder where the hell all the

souls went. There were millions of them. That kind of volume doesn't just disappear. I'm looking at one of them now like a stoned teenager, trying to piece my head together, when I hear the sound. It's a rushing sound, like a jet seconds from breaking the sound barrier. I raise my head enough to look down the river, and that's when I see the wave.

The explosion kicked everything out, but now everything is coming back, and it's coming back with force. The wave is higher than I was when I was having my pity party on top of the mesa. It's the biggest wave I've ever seen. It's a tsunami from hell.

I scramble up, forcing my limbs to get it together. I rake my hands and knees over the riverbed. I have to get to that knife. The sound is deafening, and I can feel the air sucking out like the tide would in the ocean. I throw myself toward the knife and grab it with my outstretched hand, but then I feel another hand clamp on mine. I look up; it's Douglas, his black eyes bleeding again. Then Parsons grabs it too, his eyes closed, as if feeling on instinct.

Together they raise the knife up, and I have no choice but to let them. The three of us hold the knife over the river bed as the soul wave bears down on us, and when I think I'm about to black out from the sound and the fury, I see Caroline. She's below me, through the break, like she's floating behind glass. I have to get the knife out of here. I have to get it to her. She'll know what to do, just like she did back at Chaco Rez. Just like she did with me.

I use every last ounce of strength I have to plunge the knife into the riverbed. I reach for Caroline. In my addled state, I think I actually feel her. Then the wave hits, and I lose my grip on everything.

18

CAROLINE ADAMS

I'm going to be honest with you. I took up the crow totem and joined the Circle to find Ben. That's it. There it is. That's the splat of gravy on the kitchen table. Sure, I wanted to follow the rabbit hole. Sure, I was staggered by what I'd just seen with the bell and Ben dying and the crows and my sight coming into its own. All of that made me curious, but the reason I took the crow in that parking lot was to find Ben. Just like I know Owen did it to be near me.

Joey and Big Hill said looking for the Keeper would be dangerous. They said we might even die. In my line of work, I've been in plenty of situations where the doctor or head surgeon has to deliver that type of news to a patient, and when they do, usually one of two things happens: either the patient gets it, or they flat-out don't believe it.

You'd be surprised how many people flat-out don't believe that they are in the valley of the shadow of death. It's something about humans. We never believe it can happen to us. I saw it all the time back on the oncology floor. So you'd think I'd take it seriously when the warning happened to me. But *oh, no.* I thought of the Circle's warning like you think of those travel warnings the government issues at airports. *Are you feeling ill?* Yes, always. *Please notify the TSA if you are experiencing any flu-like symptoms.* I just got off an airplane. I'm a walking flu-like symptom. *You may be at risk for the H1N1 virus.* I think I'll take my chances at home, thank you. I'm a nurse. I'd know.

In other words, it could never happen to me.

But then it does. Then you realize you're gonna die on an oil rig in Midland, Texas. And Joey Flatwood's warning rings loud in your ears, and you wonder if it was all worth it. You start to stack up your life. List it—pros and cons. But you don't have time for that, because a thin stream of fiery diesel fuel is snaking toward the blowout preventer ten feet below where you stand, and it's about to blow you and your stupid list right off the face of the earth. And you're scared shitless. So you look to your friends. And you find them looking right back at you. And then the thin scream of a rig worker stranded way up high at the top of the structure snaps you out of your inner monologue.

"Go!" he's screaming. "Run!" And you look back at Owen and you can see what he's thinking because at that moment he's the kindest, bravest, most beautiful idiot you've ever seen, and it's practically bleeding off his skin that he's going to try to save that man. He's going to tell you to run and to take Grant, and he's gonna try to maneuver his way up to the crow's nest using his totem, and he's gonna die trying to save a man he doesn't know because that's who he is. He thinks that his Hippocratic Oath somehow signed him up as a superhero and not a physician. If there's a one percent chance of saving a life, he's willing to take it. With me. With Grant. With the crows. And now with this guy, who is literally screaming at us to get away and save ourselves. The guy behind us gets it—he has a busted-up leg and he still starts shuffle-running away. But not Owen.

Owen reaches for his pocket, so I grab him. I grab him, and I kiss him. This is no little peck on the cheek, no adrenaline-fueled *let's see what it feels like* type thing, either. This one is the real deal. Now, what it means, precisely, whether I'm doing it to keep him from throwing his life away or because I'm falling for him, I don't know. That's 3:00 a.m. talk. That's not fiery-diesel-fuel-coming-at-me talk.

All I know is I want to kiss him. So I do. He freezes. His hand stops going for his pocket.

"You're staying with me," I whisper. And I pull him and Grant off the platform. With one of their hands in each of mine, I literally pull them after me, and I try to block out the screams of the poor man trapped on high. And in a lifetime of tough decisions and of dealing with those decisions, I know that this one will be the worst yet. I know those screams will tear at me forever, but I know losing Owen would tear at me more. Sometimes you have to make a goddamn choice.

We stumble down the warping metal stairs, and Grant instinctively pushes in front of us, holding the bell out straight, allowing us a chance to run into the black desert and at least giving us a fighting chance to avoid the chaos souls. I don't need to blink out to know that they are everywhere. I don't need to see the flare of the bell to know that they have saturated this place. When it blazes, Grant pulls us in another direction. We run through a minefield we can't see until Grant trips, or I trip, or maybe I'm just too exhausted to keep running, and we go down in a tumble right onto a yucca about fifty yards from the rig.

The plant slices at my arms and spears through my pants. I hit the ground hard on my wrists. I'm turned back around and facing the rig. I can see the man waving at the top, and the pain is dulled then replaced by another pain that stings me even deeper. *I'm sorry,* I think, looking at him. But I don't say it. Because that wouldn't do us any good right now. Still, I don't turn away. I feel like I owe it to the man to watch.

Owen screams something, but I'm not sure what. I'm watching the rig. And soon I have to shade my eyes, squint out to see through the blinding light of the bell. I know the souls are everywhere around us. Owen pulls me closer to Grant and tries to back away, but Grant grabs him.

"No!" Grant screams. "I have to protect you!"

"There are too many! You can't protect us. You must protect yourself. We'll be fine as long as we hold the crows!"

In a daze, I reach into my pocket and grab my crow. Owen does too. And in an instant I see that he's right. It's as if the blackest cloud of pollution you ever saw is being blended up inches from my face. The souls are barely recognizable as individual figures anymore. Only a mass of jutting hands and heads and pressing limbs. I turn to Owen, and he grabs my hand, gritting his teeth. "Hold on as long as you can," he says, his voice warped and tinny. At our backs, Grant blazes white with the protection of the bell, but it's pressed so close to him that it's basically a sheath. We'll get no more protection there.

So it's me and the crow and the pain of the thin place. The second I let go, I know I'll be smeared into paste. But already the sting of the thin place is starting, like a dull pinch. I have this bizarre flashback to elementary school when every kid had to hold a chin-up as long as they could in PE, in front of the whole class. I held my head up until my whole body shook, then I fell to the mat below. I didn't last too long.

Already my body is starting to shake with the pain. But there's no mat below me this time. Still, I can't take my eyes off the man on the rig. It's almost worse seeing him through the lens of the thin place. His soul shines brighter. It's terrified, billowing with fear but also with relief that the three of us got away. It's like a cloud around him, as if it burns twice as bright knowing it has so little time left.

Then it blinks out. Just like that, it's gone. The rig explodes. I see it as a shattering picture of greys and greens and blacks, like a great crystal sculpture blown to pieces. It doesn't so much break apart as it fragments before my eyes into a billion different shards. The flame isn't red; it's black, but I feel it like a blistering shower. I cover my face and scream, and I hear Owen and Grant do the same. But Owen never lets go of me, and Grant never scrambles or runs. He presses closer to us, as if he could still save us, and he yells for his pap.

The initial blast of heat subsides and leaves me feeling raw and sunburned, but it doesn't stop there. My teeth are ringing with the pain of the thin place, and my eyes are watery, but I can see the souls still all around us, unaffected. A thin, splattering line of black shoots high into the sky— the oil itself, pressured to blow, and it, too, is on fire. Like a live wire straight from the guts of the earth, it bellows black flames and rolling bursts of smoke into the air. Everything around us smells like burned hair and cloying oil. I'm gasping from the pain and the smells, and my knuckles are white against Owen's. He's tearing up beside me with the effort of holding his crow.

It's really hard to fight through pain when you know it's just prolonging the inevitable. I mean, if all that stands between you and death is pain, why the hell suffer pain? Everything I've ever said to the chemo patients who passed

under my care about perseverance, grit, and positive attitudes—all of it sounds so hollow to me now. My words wash
back over me, and I'm humiliated by them because I don't
think I have the soul to back them up. My grip loosens.

Then Owen clamps his free hand over mine. His face is
shaking, his brow ridged and sweating, his eyes nearly
closed, but for the first time I think it's him that's reading
me, not the other way around.

"You... never... know..." he stammers.

You never know? I want to ask him what he means, but
the pain has clamped my mouth shut as sure as if I'm being
fried in the electric chair. Why hang on?

Because Owen is hanging on. That's why.

"You... never... know... what..." Owen says again, until the
pain courses through his face and the tendons in his neck
jut out, and he throws his head back and screams, but he
still hangs on.

And then I get it. I get what he's saying. And I get it
because there's a *whoosh, pop* followed by a ripping war cry
that I swear could have come from an entire canyon full of
Navajo warriors but really comes from just one: Joey Flatwood. He's wearing nothing but leather breeches and eagle
feathers, and his face is streaked in white and dotted with
red. In his left hand he holds his crow totem. Under his right
arm, he holds the rig worker from the crow's nest. He's
carried him through the thin place, which I didn't think
possible. He drops him, unconscious, to the desert floor, and
still screaming, he lowers his head, his black hair streaming
out behind him. He hits the cloud of chaos souls like some
ancient, powerful comet that's finally swung around the
galaxy and come back for retribution. He clears through
them like a wheat thresher. His cry alone is enough to make
those nearest kick and squirm away.

It's like Owen was trying to say: you never know what one more second might bring.

I let go of my crow. Owen does the same, and we collapse onto the sand and let the warm desert night wash over us. Even the diesel-fuel-tinged air smells sweeter than an ocean breeze. We gulp it like water while around us Flatwood blinks in and out of the living world, each time with more speed and momentum than the last. Only minutes later he stands before us, dripping sweat, his muscles corded and shining bright with the distant firelight.

"*Ya'at'eeh,* Keeper!" he says, his face a jubilation. "Greetings!" Then he turns his face to the sky and screams, "They're here! Hill! Over here!"

I hear a thumping, lumbering sound, and for a second I think the rig is collapsing a second time. But then there's a *whoosh, pop,* and there in front of us, handkerchief in hand and on the verge of blubbering, is Big Hill the Bayou Bear.

"Friends!" he roars, reaching down and scooping all three of us up in his arms. He manages two seconds of a crushing hug before he starts sobbing. "I thought I'd lost you! But here you are. I knew the Walker chose true 'nuff when he said you was to guard the Keeper. And Keeper!" His blubbering reaches a new pitch. "Bah gawd, bah gawd, if it ain't you true and true," he says, as if he's known Grant for a lifetime. Grant, to his credit, is taking all of this in with wide-eyed appreciation. He nods numbly where I might have run screaming into the desert.

"The black souls regroup even now, Hill," Joey says, blinking in and out of view, as fast as lightning, and reappearing each time in a different place, his hands up and ready for a fight. Big Hill doesn't even seem to hear him. He's smiling and crying and snotting at the same time.

"Injun Joe come outta the air like thunder one day, and he says to me, he says,

'Hill, we's gatherin' the Circle,' and I says, 'Why?' And he says we gotta fight for the new kids and the Keeper, and that's all he needed to say to me 'cause I always will rememba' when the two of you stayed overn' Hill's Hill as the best time I had, and some o' the best catfishin' I ever had the privilege of fishin' was with the two of you—"

"Hill! Heads up, big man!" Joey says.

Hill looks up. "'Scuse me," he says, and he reaches into his handkerchief for his crow and blinks out. I grab my crow to watch, and Hill squares his shoulders and steps right up to a creeping line of black souls. With three swift haymaker swings, two from his right, one from his left, he belts the whole front line about twenty feet back. He turns back to us and folds his crow back away.

"Now, as I was sayin', at first when Injun Joe tells me this, I asked if you was hurt, and he said not yet but that you was fixin' to get into something soon. So this whole time I've been mixed up inside for worry. I mean, my gut wasn't right for *days* while we checked up on these thinnings. I had scuttlebutt and everything. But now we found you and—"

I think Big Hill would have gone on for a day, but he's interrupted by a spectacular cracking sound that seems to shut the whole desert up. Streaks of lightning feather the air just above our heads. Hill has to duck as tendrils of it flit right over us, and every hair on my body feels like it's doing the wave. The lightning moves toward the break, turning the desert purple.

"Hill, where are the others?" Joey asks, his voice quiet but his eyes wide and burning.

"They on their way," Hill says.

"That's good," Joey says. "We're gonna need 'em."

I hear a sound then, like the distant roar of a jet. I grab my crow and watch the lightning coalesce over the thin place, getting brighter and brighter. No more souls are dropping from the break, which should be a good thing, but in my gut I know something has gone badly wrong on the other side. A black line zips out from the break and transforms into a bird mid-flight.

"Chaco!" Grant yells, waving his hands. "We got help, Chaco! Look!"

Chaco caws three times and banks his way over to Grant. He pulls up in a whirl of feathers and settles on Grant's head. The two look at each other.

"Uh oh," Grant says, after a minute.

"What's 'uh oh'?" Owen asks. "I don't like 'uh oh.'"

"There's a wave comin'," Grant says. "Chaco says the Walker is on the other side of the thin place right now. Fighting for us. Against the agents. It's not going great."

I make a conscious effort not to look at Owen. Not to look at anything really, but I find myself peering hard into the dark, as if I could make Ben out across the veil. He's right there... but he's not. He's as far away as he ever was.

"We gotta make our way to the break," Grant says. "Be there for the Walker."

Chaco squawks loudly and caws three times.

"There are hundreds and hundreds of the souls now," I say. "And they're as thick as thieves under the break. We can't make it there ourselves. Even with Joey and Big Hill." But it's Owen I'm thinking of. Owen is the one who would throw himself into that mess headfirst. I didn't drag him out of a burning oil rig to see him off himself in a sea of black souls.

"Don't worry, Ms. Caroline," Big Hill says, rolling his

ham-hock-sized shoulders. "Ain't no member of the Circle fights alone."

"Pardon?"

Joey Flatwood walks slowly up to the front of our line. "What my redneck friend is trying to say is that we won't be doing it ourselves." He wraps the beaded lanyard of his crow tightly around his ropey forearm. The stone hangs just off his hand, ready to grab. The wave sounds like a stampede now, a thundering herd, but below it I hear another sound: *whoosh, pop!* Then another. And another as the Circle comes to our aid. A tall African woman appears at my side, and the air broken in her arrival pushes softly at my hair. She looks tribal, with a series of thin brass rings around her neck and thick bone gauges in her earlobes. She is completely bald, and when she nods, the purple light glints off her head. She faces the break and pulls a crow totem from her robes. It is wrapped loosely in a big green leaf.

There is another *whoosh, pop*, and an old man dressed in a three-piece suit walks out of thin air into the desert. He surveys the scene like we're standing on a chessboard. He turns to the break and twirls a cane in his right hand. At its top is a stone crow.

Whoosh, pop! A young man in fatigues drops a massive pack from his back and digs into the dirt with combat boots. He wears his crow around his neck, sandwiched between dog tags.

Whoosh, pop! A monk walks out of the sky like he's on a Sunday stroll and stops to set his feet on top of a small rock in a position that would have me falling right on my butt. He turns and smiles at me like a kid in a candy store, tucking his crow into the orange folds of his robes.

Whoosh, pop! A woman in a pantsuit and wearing high

heels steps into the desert sand and sinks three inches. She steps out of them and with a gloved hand drops her crow into a designer clutch she carries at her side. She winks at me.

Again and again it's like this. Ten, eleven, twelve times. An Australian aboriginal lands twenty feet to my left and swipes a wide and perfect circle around himself with his right toe. His crow is in his hair; it seems to glow in the moonlight, wrapped in messy dreads. A small man wearing an animal pelt and with a beard so long and thick it obscures everything but his eyes steps out nearby. His crow peeks out near his chin, through his beard. He unclasps a coat that looks to be made of the wool of at least ten sheep and lets it fall to the ground before he screams bloody murder at the blackness underneath the break. I lose count of all those that arrive, each of them unique. Some elegant, some wild, but all dangerous. And all of them with one goal in mind: protecting the bell. And to do that, we gotta close that break.

The *we* strikes me as absurd. I have no place among these people, right? I mean, we've got warriors here. I'm a neurotic nurse. Not even a nurse anymore, technically. More of a neurotic RVer. I look over at Owen. He's too open mouthed to even look back, so I know he's feeling the same thing. But something about the way each Circle member nods at us settles me. It's like we're already part of the team. Like we're at a big, crazy family reunion at the end of the world.

"*Ya'at'eeh*, Circle!" Joey cries. "Welcome! We fix the break today." It's not a question. Not an entreaty. It's a fact. We're *going* to fix the break. "We fight for the bell. We fight for the Walker. We fight for *this* place. This is *our* place." Joey scoops up some desert dust with his hand and sprinkles it over his head. He spits in his hand and wipes the paste under his eyes.

"Our place," he says again. He turns to the break. "We go."

Just like that. Not a pep talk for the ages, perhaps, but one that rings true. I know because anything that makes me want to reach up and rub dirt on my own face must be persuasive. I hate dirt.

Joey starts to run, and before he hits his second stride, he lets loose another ripping war cry of the sort I'm going to go ahead and say hasn't been heard for centuries. It's a thing taken from the top shelf of his people, dusted off, and pumped full of nitro gas. It would have sent a whole army of men running, but these things aren't men any longer. I find myself sprinting at them. Owen is right beside me, the Circle to both sides, and Grant at our heels clutching the bell in his hand. We run at them like our own rushing wave.

The chaos souls are actually drawn to us. I think they feel the energy, the coordination of the attack, and the unity of purpose, and they want to ruin it. So they come at us, and even with this crew, I can't see a way to get through the masses of black. But that's before I see how hard the Circle hits. It's the spinning cane of the older man that I see first. He's doesn't seem so old now, though, and his crow blurs in a turquoise circle like it's a flaming blue staff. When it hits the chaos souls, it shreds them like an airplane propeller. They are blown to black dust that is sucked back up and away.

Joey Flatwood is a force of nature. He walks through the thin place like it's his own personal garden and he's pruning dead leaves. He looks more at home here than he does in the real world. The souls he hits are turned into Rorschach inkblots with the force of his fists. Even so, he's leading this charge, and there's a terrible moment where he's separated from the rest of us. The oily black pools around the back of him, and suddenly he's on an island. The bald woman yells and points, but it's too late. They're all around him, and even Joey can't guard the blind side of his back. Owen throws himself forward and lowers his shoulder into the souls, but he's thrown back. I can only watch as they reach for Joey's grip on his crow and manage to pry it away finger by finger. He fights like a bull but can't hold on and blinks back. A soul swipes at his chest, and its fingers rake into him, pulling flesh like sand. He screams and rips his crow back, blinking back in time to save himself, but he drops to the ground.

Big Hill is there. He is a human cannonball. A rolling boulder. He plows his way through the souls and reaches Joey. He picks him up like he's made of straw and sets him on his feet. He's frantic, crying and seething at the same time.

Joey shakes his head and pats Big Hill's chest. I see him nod. I am more relieved by this than perhaps anything that has happened to me on this insane day. The rest of the Circle sees Joey rise again, and a wild cheer goes up. We redouble our efforts. A host of different war cries washes over the desert, and all around me the turquoise crows glow bright in the hollow darkness of the desert in the thin place. The burn of holding the crow seems to lessen.

Grant walks past me as cool as a cucumber with Chaco bobbing along on his head. The souls shy away from him. He takes up my hand at the last second and tugs me along through a sea of chaos. I try to pull him back, but he's not having it. He shakes his head again and again.

Chaco screeches louder than I've ever heard him. The sound itself makes the press of souls back off. Grant nods in agreement. Grant says, "We only got one shot at this."

"One shot at what?" I ask. "And if you've only got one shot at a thing, maybe you should get Joey or somebody else. Anybody else."

Grant shakes his head. "Not Joey."

"Then get Owen." My mouth is dry, really dry. Not just because of the war going on around me but because I know where he's taking me. He's taking me right under the break. "Owen!" I scream.

Owen looks up from where he's attending to Joey's wound while Big Hill gives them cover. He makes toward us, but Grant shakes his head.

"Not Owen," Grant says. He tugs me along harder. Chaco turns and looks at me. He's right at my eye level, and he's doing that bird thing where his body moves with every step Grant takes, but his head stays dead still.

"We don't have much time," Grant says, pulling me faster. Now we're really in the thick of it. Grant blazes like a lighthouse, but I'm not so immune. They pull at me and go for my crow, so I tuck it under my armpit and throw my elbows like I'm breaking down a door just to take each step. Now that we're this near the break, I can hear the wave again, and it's like how I'd imagine sticking my head under the hood of a semi-truck barreling down a mountain might sound. I can see up and through it now, and there on the other side I see the faint outline of three bodies. Two of them are bone white and dressed in suits. The other is Ben. They aren't moving. This evidently pisses Chaco off, because he caws about as loud as I've ever heard him caw. They shift a little bit. In the middle of the three of them sits the knife. The air smokes and bubbles around it.

We're right underneath the break now. No more souls drop through, but I know they're coming. They're coming on the crest of that tsunami I'm hearing. It's all I can hear now.

The sound is so loud it's become a physical thing that vibrates my teeth and tries to push me back.

"He has to wake up. He has to get to the knife," Grant says, his voice dazed, his head cricked back all the way like he's stargazing. Chaco is staring at me. Then Grant turns to look at me too. "Chaco says you need to call him."

"Ben!" I shout. "Ben! It's me! It's Caroline! Please, Ben. You gotta get the knife."

He moves.

"Ben! Can you... can you hear me?"

The break is getting bigger. Pieces of the ground Ben lies on flake off and shift to smoke above us. I think of the last time I spoke to Ben. Of the kiss before he walked away from his body, away from me forever. They call him the Walker, but I remember the man who was dying from cancer and from the chemo that we used to try and kill it, vomiting in his back yard, giving everything he had left to try and find some closure for his family, for himself.

"Ben, we need you," I say. "I need you."

He shakes his head a bit and rolls onto his back. He's coming back, slowly. Unfortunately, so are the agents. Douglas is the fastest to orient himself. And to remember the knife. He reaches for it, and I see in his scarred face that he is intent on using it on Ben. But Ben grabs it at the same time. Ben has a better grip on the knife, and I think he's going to yank it free until Parsons makes a grab too. Then Ben is overmatched. My heart slumps. And that's when Ben sees me.

The sound is a high-pitched keening roar now. The three of them look like they're in a vacuum. Their clothes and hair are pulled back toward the force bearing down on them, and the agents' ties flip and turn. The wave is pulling everything out before it slams back in. Ben's black hair flutters out over his eyes, but he's looking at me, and I really see him for the first time in almost a year.

I wave.

I know. It's a stupid thing to do, but it's the only thing I can think of. So I wave at him like a ten-year-old girl saying hello to her grandparents. His mouth opens a little so that I think he may start to smile, but the agents yank at the knife. Whatever smile there was turns into a grimace as he strains to keep control.

"Catch," he says. Or I think he says it. I read it on his lips. All three hands slam down on the break. The knife slips through and tumbles from the sky, glinting green as it falls as if in slow motion, spinning end over end. The agents follow it, reaching and falling through themselves, grasping after it like it's a golden coin dropped in the ocean. I step back from it, terrified to touch the blade.

Joey Flatwood catches it out of midair. His hand strikes out like a cobra, and he snatches it right by the hilt, one handed, despite his bleeding chest. The wave of souls is almost on top of Ben. I can see it like a skyscraper above him.

He reaches out for me. Reaches through the break. His hand comes through, floats in midair. I reach up and touch his finger. I swear I touch his finger. I'm not making this up. I know because it's not like I just feel the smoke of a ghost. I feel the rough fold of his knuckle and the smooth slip of his nail. Real things. He smiles at me. It's a sad smile. It's not the smile of a man who is coming back. It's the smile of a man who knows he has to go away.

Then the wave hits him, and his arm is snapped back, and he's gone in a blink. The sky shudders with a long, low rumble of thunder, and it feels like the very air is weighted down on our heads like a balloon seconds from bursting.

Joey Flatwood takes the knife, jams it between two rocks at our feet, takes a big jump in the air, and lands square on the handle with both heels.

The blade snaps with a crack like lightning. The chaos souls are blown to dust and sucked instantly away. Every member of the Circle takes cover, expecting the thin place to blow apart, but the shattering doesn't come. Nothing comes. The sky eases back into itself, straightening, flattening. The break starts to knit, layers and layers of shining thread moving over and through the patch in the sky until there's nothing but the faint, vague thinning that made this stretch of desert what it is in the first place.

I don't know how long I stand staring at the empty sky. There is movement all around me, the men and women of the Circle calling roll and tending to their own injuries. I must look like a lost kid in a supermarket, but I don't care. I want to try to remember that touch. I want to think about it for a while.

Eventually Owen brings me back. He taps me lightly on the shoulder. I turn to him. He doesn't speak. No hint of anger or jealousy mars his smoke. They might have been there once, but not anymore. Now there is understanding. And worry. And love. And a question that I don't give him time to ask, because he shouldn't have to. Not anymore. I lay my head against his chest, and he holds me.

"I love you, Owen," I say. But Owen surprises me.

"I'm not so sure you do, Caroline."

I look up at him, my brow furrowed. My mouth works, but nothing comes out. He just laughs and presses his lips to my forehead. Not a kiss, exactly, but something kinder. Something better.

"I don't know what we've got, you and I," he says. "But I'm willing to take a lifetime to figure it out."

I nod, pressing my cheek to his chest. "Me too."

"And what about these two crazies?" Grant asks, standing over by the agents, who lie still on the desert floor. Chaco squawks loudly.

"Get away from them, Grant," Owen says and reaches for his hand. He pulls him over to us. "They'll kill you as soon as look at you just to get that bell."

Grant squints at them. "I dunno. I think they might be... broken."

I creep forward with my hands raised like I expect the agents to pull a jack-in-the-box at any second, but when I get close enough to see their faces clearly, I think Grant may be right. They aren't dead, but they aren't with us, either. Their eyes are closed, but their faces look like they're being forced to watch something horrible. Douglas twitches minutely, almost as if he's trying to shake his head. Parsons's eyes flit wildly underneath their pale, black-veined lids. His mouth looks like it wants to turn down but can't.

"They both look like they want to cry or something," Grant says.

Joey Flatwood circles around and watches them with his arms crossed over his chest. His wound seems not to bother him at all. In fact, it sort of goes with his look, like a wolf or maybe a bear swiped a claw across his pec right before Joey kicked its ass. And that's not too far from the truth.

"It's the knife," Joey says. "They put too much of themselves into it. When it broke, so did they."

I know I should throw out a "serves them right" and walk away. These two have put us through unrelenting hell for a year now. Parsons tried to kill me, and nearly did kill Owen. They're lunatics. Obsessive. They walked over us in their quest for the bell and would do it all again if they had the chance. I try to turn away and leave them for the coyotes and the rattlesnakes, I really do, and I'm sure if I were the first to turn away, the others would follow. Even now Joey looks at me, and his smoke says, *Your kill.*

But it's not in me. I surprise myself by kneeling down over Parsons, and before I know it, I'm sweeping over him with my other sight. I've never been this close to the agents without being afraid for my life, and now that they're here, I can see that they still smoke. Meaning they're not dead. Meaning they still have souls somewhere in there. Parsons's smoke is black, true, but it's a broken black now. I scoop some of it up, and it pools in my hand. I look carefully at it. There is definitely another color in there, underneath the black. I see flashes of it, like a gemstone buried in mud. It's a soft yellow. Not unlike Owen's was when I first met him. Professional. Straightforward. Meticulous.

I picture the yellow in my mind and all the things that yellow could represent. A man with a job he was proud of. A man who worked hard. Perhaps too hard. A man who was swallowed up in something but before that might have been like us. And with all this in my mind, I blow on the smoke in my hand... and the black dissipates a little. And with it, the pulsing twitch at Parsons's temple calms.

I know what I have to do.

I move around Parsons to his head, where I see his smoke at its root. I'm not sure how the soul works or where it leads, but I see a clear connection here to the other plane in everyone, and Parsons's is still roiling in broken black smoke. I put my hand on his forehead, and I hear Owen stir. He wants to come take me away from this man. He took a bullet from this man for me once. I look up at him and smile.

"I can do this," I say. "It's what I do."

He calms himself with a big breath and crosses his arms. Chaco watches me carefully but nods.

I picture the yellow again. Parsons's yellow. Driven, practical, meticulous, perhaps overbearing. But pure, uncorrupted. Then I place my hand over his face and brush upward toward his forehead. It's a strange, plucking sensation, like I'm pulling a rotten sheaf from a head of corn, but underneath is the pure yellow. And with each inch, his tremors still, and before my eyes, his color returns. The white fills in, the black veins fade away. With one last push, I dissipate the black smoke fully, and it falls away entirely.

He calms. His body stills, relaxes into the warm desert floor. He takes a big, shuddering breath. Then he opens his eyes. They are clear and green. Owen steps forward along with Joey Flatwood, but I hold up my hand. They pause.

"Parsons?" I ask, my voice barely above a whisper. His eyes find me and focus then blink. He takes me in then turns his head and marks each of us surrounding him. He pushes up onto his elbows, and I step back a little bit. He rubs at his face and his eyes, then he looks back at me.

"Who the hell are you people? And what have you done to me?"

"It's a long story," I say. I try not to smile, since I know that would probably seem creepy to a man who just woke up from a nightmare to find himself in the desert surrounded by a strange host that includes an Indian, a man as big as a hill, and a boy with a crow on his head.

He looks over at his partner, still on the ground, still twitching.

"Allen?" he asks, trying to get up and nearly collapsing. "Hey! Allen!" He turns to me, frantic. "Is he okay? What have you done to him?"

"He'll be fine, soon enough. We didn't do anything to

him. We're here to help you. What is the last thing you remember, Parsons? Think back to the last thing you did. What case you were on."

Parsons looks strangely at me. "Case?"

"Yes, you were tracking a man named Joey Flatwood. You thought he was running drugs."

"Flatwood? Drugs? What the hell are you talking about? Allen and I are archivists."

"Get the fuck outta here," Owen blurts out in the dead silence that follows. I glare at him. He coughs. "Sorry, it's just... you guys? Librarians?"

"Not librarians, *archivists*." Parsons stands slowly and dusts his hands off. He walks carefully over to Douglas, and I see the worry in his eyes. He gasps at the scarred claw marks that rake Douglas's face. I move over to Douglas and start focusing to find his hidden color. I hear Owen talking in the background of my mind.

"It's just that we thought you guys were FBI agents. You had badges and suits. And you were pretty handy with a gun," he says. "For a librarian."

I see Douglas's color. It's a pale blue. I almost think I have it wrong, because what I see is a kind-hearted man, gentle, not at all in line with the brutish thug I know. If anything, he is too meek. Too soft-spoken. The type of man who would take easily to being told what to do. I focus on that color and push away his darkness. He comes back to us by degrees just like Parsons did. Even the scars on his face fade, although they don't disappear altogether.

Parsons drops to his side and grabs his hand. "Allen? Can you hear me, Allen?"

Douglas opens his eyes. They are clear and blue, not unlike his smoke color, with no hint of the trauma that left him bloody. The hard lines of his face are gone. The scars are soft pink. His entire person has softened.

"James? What happened?" He slowly sits up, with our help. He looks all around him at the desert night. "Where are all the books? Oh, dear. Did I have too much wine again?"

Parsons pauses. He looks over at me, still holding Douglas's hand. "That's it. Books. We were at work. We do work for the government but not like you think. We're senior archivists at the Library of Congress. Which I take it is not anywhere near where we are right now."

"You're in the west Texas desert," Grant says.

"That's a long way from the stacks in DC," Owen adds.

"Yes!" Parsons says. "The stacks! We were retrieving a book in the restricted stacks! It was a little thing, almost like a lady's black book or something. A strange thing. It was unmarked..."

"Yes," Douglas says, nodding. "It was an old, leatherbound book. I remember pulling it from the stacks, and taking it from its sheath, and handing it to you, and... that's it."

"I tried to read it, to check it was the correct volume, but every page was blank. I felt very odd, though, like the words were just out of sight. Looking at it made me feel a little ill, so I put it away. And then I heard something. Something calling my name. I *felt* something. Right there with us. And..."

"And?" Owen prompts.

"And that's it. Just like Allen. Here I am. In the desert. With a splitting headache."

Each of us mutters a curse in our own way. We were that close. Whatever it was Parsons and Douglas retrieved, it is the key to understanding this whole thing. The attack on the veil. The knife. Their obsessive mission. All of it. Without it, we're just shell-shocked survivors of a battle we don't quite understand. I see the colors around me, the smoke of the Circle, dampened by disappointment. Only Grant seems undaunted.

"Well, where did you put it away?" he asks.

Parsons looks over at him, at the crow on his head, and blinks. "Put it away?"

"The book. You said you put it away. Before the other thing came up on ya."

"Yes..." Parsons pats at his pants pockets, then his jacket pockets, then reaches into his breast pocket. He freezes.

"Oh, shit," he says, his eyes wide. He slowly pulls his hand out, and in his grasp is a small, leather-bound book, black as night, about the size of an address book. "I took it from the stacks," he whispers.

All of us stare at it. Chaco shivers his feathers. I sense no power in the book itself, no malice, but it is a heavy thing, despite its size. It has weight to it that spans across the planes, just like the bell, although if the bell is like solid silver, this is like solid lead.

The book might look blank to others but not to me. Its title is written in smoke that I can see quite clearly. It says *The Book of the Dark Walker*.

"Oooh, James," Douglas says quietly. "You are *so* fired."

19

THE WALKER

I'm gonna let you in on a little secret.

I wanted the knife for myself.

Yes, I know it was ripped unwilling from the vein of the earth. Yes, I know that the turquoise was perverted when the agents hammered and chipped it into a weapon. Yes, I am aware that it nearly destroyed the balance between the living world, the thin world, and the world of the dead. All of this I know.

But it was a key. It was my way out, back into the land of the living, if I so chose. Not sayin' I would choose that, but it'd be nice to have in my back pocket. The whole time I was getting my ass kicked by Douglas then stranded on top of the mesa then chasing after the agents down the river, in the back of my mind I was thinking, *How can I get these assholes out of here but keep that knife?*

Then Caroline looked at me, and all that went out the window. That's all it took to give it up for the greater good. She looked at me, and I *think* she even touched me. I knew then the only way I could stop the balance from breaking and the world from spinning out of control was to give her the knife. So I did. Like a prisoner who finally snatches the cell keys from the wall then decides to chuck them out the window.

At least I didn't have long to think about it. A tsunami of souls smashing into your body will do that to you. Back at Chaco Rez, we'd usually get one or two big snowstorms every winter, and afterward Gam, Mom, and Dad would take Ana and me to this place south of the Arroyo where the basin leveled out but there was still a good-sized hill for sledding. We'd drive through the Arroyo proper to pick up Joey, and Gam would stop by to check on a few people. At the time I thought this was just her seeing friends, but looking back on it, I think Gam wanted to make sure the Arroyo old-timers survived the storm, which wasn't a given back then and ain't a given now either. Then they'd set up camp at the top of the hill with the other families and watch the three of us kids sled and sled and sled. I mean hundreds of times. All day long. And every time we'd make sure they were watching, and they'd wave and then go back to their knitting or their beers or their magazines.

Ana was just little, so she couldn't do much more than roll around and slide a little down the hill, but Joey and I built big jumps and competed with each other for who could take the one good tube down the hill fastest and get the biggest air. One time we built a kicker too well. This thing was perfect. Joey wanted to be the first down, but I grabbed the tube from him and got a running start and everything just came together. I was flying. Then I hit the kicker and basically rag-dolled. I lost my gloves before I even hit the ground, and when I did hit, I lost my boots and my hat and my jacket ripped open. I was spinning and spinning and spinning, and then all of a sudden I couldn't breathe, there was a huge thump, and everything went white.

That's what it was like when the wave of souls hit me. If I had gloves, they'd be halfway across the world right now. If I had a hat, it would be in another dimension. On the hill, turns out I couldn't breathe because I had snow in my throat, and everything went white because I was stuck ass up in a big drift at the bottom. My throat opened after a panicked half minute, and Joey was there to pull me out of the drift. Gam patched me up. We kept sledding.

This time what chokes me is the weight of billions of individual images. The imprints of thousands upon thousands of souls. I'm crushed by them without them ever weighing me down, and this time there's nobody to pull me out. The pure emotional attack is too much even for me to take—and I walk a map of souls for a job. Thankfully I still have that fail-safe off switch: eventually I just black out.

When I come around again, I'm back in the cavern. The wash has driven me all of the way down and under again. I'm floating around like a dead fish near the top, where the pearl is connected to the eggcup by that long strand. I actually bump my head against the pearl. It's what wakes me up, and it's not forgiving.

When I look around, it seems to me like everything is back to normal. The souls have settled in their own way and are back to their slow spinning circle around the pearl, and after blinking and rubbing my face to get some sense back, I kick off toward the inlet where the river lets off. Two visits to this weird-ass chaos globe are plenty for me. I'd be perfectly fine never seeing this place again.

It's only when I chance a look back over my shoulder to see the whole of the cavern one last time that I notice that things are definitely *not* back to normal. As a matter of fact, things may never be normal again.

The pearl has split wide open. I couldn't see it from the back, but it's opened like a massive clam from the front, right down the seam where the knife blew through those locks. I sort of float there, staring at it for a minute. Once I'm reasonably sure it's not gonna blow up on me again, I swim toward it.

I stop at the edge of the pearl. The shiny veneer is pretty thin, actually, only an arm's length or so deep on a thing the size of a domed football stadium. The rest of it looks like it's made up of thick, black coral pitted and grooved with tiny rivulets and pathways, almost like veins, leading from the outside inward.

I look back toward the inlet, where the shore lies just beyond. Nothing but floating silence out there. I look back inward, to the center of the pearl. Nothing but floating silence in there, either. And when you're stuck between two empty places, you'd be surprised how willing you are to check out the one you haven't seen. Even if it is spooky. Either way, whatever the agents wanted is in here. I'm not leaving until I figure out what it is.

I kick along with one hand lightly touching the inner wall. I get sensations from the touch that are sort of like when a soul hits me but less powerful, more diluted. As if these thousands of capillaries etched along the inside of the pearl are sifting the emotions and echoes, refining them. The grooves get bigger the deeper I go. Soon they are the thickness of my arm, then my leg, then my whole body. When I see a vein the size of a car, I start to sweat. This thing is looking more and more like the shell of a living creature. I kick harder, shooting toward the center. The veins get bigger and bigger, and soon they're the size of a school bus... and then they stop.

By now the light from the souls floating around outside is very weak, so it takes me a second to see what happened. The main veins collapse very quickly into a hundred different cones. The cones start wide, but they narrow fast, and as I swim forward, I see them for what they are. Needles. They're essentially needles that channel the chaos souls from the outside, refine them, and then shoot them right to the center.

I want out of here.

I'm tearing forward to see what's there, then I'm getting out. This whole place is messing with me, scattering my thoughts. I can hardly keep moving in a straight line. Even the echo of what was here is enough to muddle my brain. I focus on swimming. I focus on things I know. Ana, Joey, Owen, Caroline.

And then I'm there. I'm at the center of the pearl. And what finally makes me turn around, what makes me hightail my ass out of there at double the clip I went in, isn't that I find what the agents wanted. It's that I find nothing at all.

Literally, I find a hollow. But it's a hollow in the shape of a person. All the chaos energy from all the souls that have ever existed gets shot into here. Right into this hollow. And the hollow is empty.

The locks weren't set on the pearl to keep something from getting in. They were set to keep something from getting out.

And now it's out.

I'M FOLLOWING footprints in the sand, and they aren't mine. I noticed them as soon as I kicked my way out of the river of

souls and got back to the beach. At first they were hard to
follow because the ever-changing landscape at the chaos end
of the river messed around with their placement. The earth
shifted under me, and I lost them for a time. But I reasoned
that whatever came out of the pearl was on its way down the
beach, so I ran, figuring I'd pick them up again after I got out
of the crazy fun-house nightmare of the chaos end of things.

I was right. Now that the riverbank is more level and the
world isn't bucking under me, I can see that the footprints
are human. Look to be male. The gait is such that it's a tall
guy, or a man running, but the pressure points don't suggest
running. Just a big fella with a big stride.

Just when I'm about to congratulate myself for the old
cop instincts kicking in, the footprints change. I don't mean
change pace. I mean they change entirely. Now they're children's footprints, barely bigger than the palm of my hand,
and they indicate a quick step. Then, impossibly, the tiny
footprints space farther and farther apart until this child is
walking with the gait of a giant. Then something bigger
than a giant. Then they change again. I stop and stare at the
print where the change happens. The front half is the print
of a child's toes. The back half is a hoof. I stare at that one
for a while. The next print is a full-on hoof. Then the hoof-
prints are spaced wildly apart.

Then come the claw prints. I break out in a cold sweat at
these. No way around it. They give me the shivers, which is
why I nearly bury my head in the sand when I hear a snapping sound and see a dark line shoot out of the river like an
obsidian spear chucked from below. I'm seriously halfway
dug in with my feet before I realize it's just Chaco. He spies
me and soars my way.

"Hate to cut your vacation short, Walker," he says, "but

there are, like, a hundred thousand souls backed up in the pipes here, man, and you gotta get back to work."

"How'd you get here? I thought I sealed the break. Not that I'm not overjoyed to see you."

"I'm a thinning. I can travel through all thin places. I don't need no stinkin' break. But seriously, what the hell are you waiting for? The veil is almost back to one hundred percent..."

He trails off as he gets closer to me and sees the dark imprints of the tracks. This claw print would be hard to miss, even from the air. He flutters down to my shoulder, and we stare at them for a second.

"Who let the dinosaur in?" Chaco says, finally.

I point my finger down the way I came. "Dinosaur-thing, goat-thing, demon-spawn child-thing, big-ass man-thing. Lots of things."

"And one thing," Chaco says. We follow the trail in silence. The claws dig huge rivets in the sand... until they don't. About a hundred yards down, they change into a man's footprint again in a single step. They continue for another ten paces, then they disappear. I look at Chaco, and he takes off, shooting down the beach toward dead center, where I left the veil. He flies for a time, sweeping low, his head snapping this way and that, as if he's looking for a mouse to eat. He goes on down until I can't see him anymore. Then, after a time, he comes back. He pumps his wings to gain speed then flares out right before me to plop on my shoulder again.

"Nothing," he says.

"What? What do you mean nothing?"

"I mean nothing. Nada. Zilch. No more tracks. Not at the veil, not past the veil, not anywhere."

"You're telling me this thing just disappeared?"

Chaco is eyeing the tracks with unblinking bird focus. "He didn't use the veil. And he didn't cross over through a thin place, because I would know. So... yeah. He pretty much disappeared. I don't get it."

"Great. I thought you got everything. That's been our MO. I fuck around and nearly destroy the world, and you patch it all up after me with your timeless wisdom."

"You fuck around with the best of intentions, of course," Chaco says, absently.

"Of course."

"Where the hell did this thing come from, Walker?"

"A big pearl in the chaos eggshell."

"Say what?"

"It came from inside a big black pearl at the chaos end of the river."

Chaco snaps his head back to me. "What did you say?" He sounds deadly serious. "Did you say a big black pearl?"

"Yes, bird. That's what I'm saying."

He walks slowly along my shoulder until he is inches from me, then he tilts his beak down and walks closer until his feathered head and beady eyes are centimeters from mine.

"I want to be very clear here. Super-duper clear. This thing came from inside the black pearl? You're sure of it?"

I've tilted my head back as far as it goes, but Chaco doesn't move. He stares me down.

"Yes! The agents broke the locks to the pearl with the knife. It blew us out of the chamber when they broke. We fought for the knife on the riverbed, and I tossed it through. The tsunami hit me, and I blacked out. When I came to, I was back in the chamber. The pearl was open. I swam inside to have a look around and found a sort of sarcophagus thing that looked like it once held a man. I swam out here and found these tracks."

Chaco stares at me for a good ten seconds.

"So what is it?" I ask.

"I don't know." That's twice now Chaco has been stumped, and it feels as unnatural as these claw prints look. "The pearls anchor the river. Chaos on one side and order on the other. It's been that way since the dawn of time. Since before the dawn of time, actually, because I came around at the dawn of time, when the river started wearing away at its banks and bed, which rivers will do, and created the first thinning. Yours truly."

"So this thing is... older than you?"

"I didn't even know there was a *thing* there. I've only ever seen the pearls. I thought they were just inanimate lightning rods for their respective types of souls. Maybe inside was millions of years of soul goo. That's it. It never occurred to me that an entity could be in there. Much less an entity that makes tracks like this."

"So we know where it came from," I say, trying to talk through things, to order them in my mind and keep me from running around doing something stupid—which is usually what happens when I panic. "The next question would be—"

"Where the hell did it go?" Chaco says, taking the words from my mouth.

And this is one question that shuts us both up.

I GET BACK through the veil. Actually, the veil seems all too eager to get me back on the other side of it where I belong. It basically pulls me in and through itself once I get within arm's length of where it billows at the middle of the river, robustly red once more. I fall out on my ass in the middle of the desert, right where the thick of the mess happened. I see the whole gang still here, patching themselves up, gathering themselves, but once again, I'm in my own world. They can't see me, they can't hear me, and they can't touch me.

Yep. The good ol' days are back again.

The first thing I notice is that the agents don't look like the agents anymore. They look more like overworked accountants, and they're talking to the Circle members like they've never seen anything like them before. I know immediately that this is Caroline's doing. That she fixed them or helped them in some way, because that's what she does, what she was made for.

Then I find Caroline. She stands next to Owen. He has his arm around her shoulder. Between them is Grant, and I don't need to case the place to realize that the Keeper has a new family now.

I try to get jealous. I try to get pissed. I can't do either. But I do ache. My body aches, and my heart aches. I don't begrudge Owen anything. That man has been a class act since day one. But I do begrudge his arm. The arm that he has resting around Caroline when mine would pass right through her. It's the little things that get to you.

Chaco is already resting on Grant's head. "He's right over there," Chaco says, nudging his beak my way. Grant stares into the open space that is me on the side of the living, and he gives a small wave. He smiles, too. It's an awesome smile. I wave back, even though I know damn well he can't see me.

Caroline asks him who he's waving to. "Nobody," he says. Which tells me he's more perceptive than I thought. That maybe he figured out about this whole mess of hearts without anyone saying anything and doesn't want to get involved. But Caroline knows. She looks my way too, and she smiles. It's exhausted and a little sad, but it's genuine. It hits me that she's sad for me. Caroline feels sorry for me.

If you ever want to light a fire under a Navajo's ass, or under any red-blooded man's ass, really, all you gotta do is tell them you feel sorry for them.

I straighten up. I roll my shoulders back until I hear a crack. I ball my fists. Chaco looks at me and puffs up as well.

I got work to do. I got souls to settle. Then I got a monster to find.

And since you've been along for this whole ride so far, I might as well stick with the honesty thing. I want to find this creepy Other Walker for two reasons: First, because I want to right the balance of the river. It won't do to have millions of souls swirling around an empty pearl for too much longer. Even I know that.

Second, because I want to see what it is. Specifically, how it can just flit in and out of worlds. And I've got a completely selfish motive for this one. I've got a strong hunch, a near certain hunch, that this thing, whatever it is, is walking the world of the living.

And if it can walk with the living, maybe one day I can too.

ABOUT THE AUTHOR

B. B. Griffith writes best-selling fantasy and thriller books. He lives in Denver, CO, where he is often seen sitting on his porch staring off into the distance or wandering to and from local watering holes with his family.

See more at his digital HQ: bbgriffith.com

If you like his books, you can sign up for his mailing list here: http://eepurl.com/SObZj. It is an entirely spam-free experience.

ALSO BY B. B. GRIFFITH

The Vanished Series

Follow the Crow (Vanished, #1)

Beyond the Veil (Vanished, #2)

The Coyote Way (Vanished, #3)

Gordon Pope Thrillers

The Sleepwalkers (Gordon Pope, #1)

Mind Games (Gordon Pope, #2)

Shadow Land (Gordon Pope, #3)

The Tournament Series

Blue Fall (The Tournament, #1)

Grey Winter (The Tournament, #2)

Black Spring (The Tournament, #3)

Summer Crush (The Tournament, #4)

Luck Magic Series

Las Vegas Luck Magic (Luck Magic, #1)

Standalone

Witch of the Water: A Novella

Made in the USA
Monee, IL
01 February 2021

59309510R00125